JAGUARS' TOMB

ANGÉLICA GORODISCHER

Jaguars' Tomb

Translated by Amalia Gladhart

Vanderbilt University Press
NASHVILLE, TENNESSEE

Library of Congress Cataloging-in-Publication Data

Names: Gorodischer, Angélica, author. | Gladhart, Amalia, translator.
Title: Jaguars' tomb / Angélica Gorodischer ; translated by Amalia
  Gladhart.
Other titles: Tumba de jaguares. English
Description: Nashville : Vanderbilt University Press, [2021] | Includes
  bibliographical references.
Identifiers: LCCN 2020039751 (print) | LCCN 2020039752 (ebook) | ISBN
  9780826501400 (paperback) | ISBN 9780826501417 (hardcover) | ISBN
  9780826501424 (epub) | ISBN 9780826501431 (pdf)
Classification: LCC PQ7798.17.O73 T8613 2021 (print) | LCC PQ7798.17.O73
  (ebook) | DDC 863/.64—dc23

LC record available at https://lccn.loc.gov/2020039751
LC ebook record available at https://lccn.loc.gov/2020039752

To Goro, as always;
to my friend Hilda Rais, poet.

CONTENTS

TRANSLATOR'S ACKNOWLEDGMENTS

Work on this translation was supported by a Translation Fellowship from the National Endowment for the Arts, for which I am most grateful. Thanks also to W. Andrew Marcus, then Tykeson Dean of the College of Arts and Sciences, University of Oregon, for a grant from the dean's discretionary funds to support research and travel to Argentina. I presented work in progress at several ALTA (American Literary Translators Association) conferences, benefitting from the input of knowledgeable and generous audiences. Translator friends provided needed sounding-boards and offered numerous suggestions; thanks especially to the "Ashland Translators": Priscilla

Hunter, Amanda Powell, Karen McPherson, Suzanne Jill Levine, and Susanne Petermann. It has been a privilege to work with Angélica Gorodischer, on this and other projects, enjoying her good humor, hospitality, conversation, and friendship—mil gracias, y un fuerte abrazo. Deepest gratitude, as ever, to my family, for their supportive curiosity, patience, and good company.

INTRODUCTION
Octagonal Rooms
Writing, Absence, Translation, Play

Amalia Gladhart

Tumba de jaguares (*Jaguars' Tomb*), first published in 2005, is a novel in three linked parts, each attributed to a different, fictional novelist. Angélica Gorodsicher's novel is both an intriguing puzzle and a meditation on how to write about, or through, violence, injustice, and loss. The novel plays with the repetitive possibilities of words and images, and raises questions about representation and writing, about whether art can offer refuge or resolution, and about the extent to which a writer's authority must derive from experience rather than imagination. Two of the writers in the novel are women, one at the beginning of her career, one at the end. Two women writing, or possibly three: Gorodischer observes in an interview, cited by Diana Battaglia, "Somos cuatro los que escribimos: las dos mujeres, el hombre, y yo" (Battaglia 138; There are four of us who write: the two women, the man, and myself).[1] As Guillermo Saccomanno wrote in an early review of the novel, Gorodischer "plantea la escritura como antídoto que en lugar de cicatrizar la ausencia, la exacerba" (posits writing as an antidote that, rather than scarring over absence, exacerbates it). There are links to an Argentine reality (such as subtle but clear allusions to the Madres de la Plaza de Mayo), yet the "where" of the novel is a more ambiguous, even generic literary geography; the writers who populate the novel navigate the commonplaces of those literary landscapes in an effort to either express or evade (sometimes both) the violations and absences that have shaped their individual experiences and that motivate their writing. The tension between experience and imagination underlies the writers' different approaches to the unsayable, to borrowed pain, to the fascination of a horror they both want to and cannot avoid, that which perhaps ought not to be said, even as it must not be forgotten.

Jaguars' Tomb produces a sensation of beginning, middle, and end. And yet, while it is possible to read the final section as the culmination, the "true" origin of the events described in the other sections, it, too, is a doubly fictitious text. The last part of

---

1 In a later interview with Adrián Ferrero, Gorodischer reflects—with her customary humor—on her own writing career, in the early years working around the demands of home and family, later with more time and space to herself: "No me arrepiento: yo quería todo, hijos, marido, casa, una familia y escribir. A los tumbos, a los ponchazos, como se pudiera, pero lo conseguí y a veces, cuando me doy permiso, me siento orgullosa. No se lo digas a nadie." (Ferrero, "Entrevista" 36; I'm not sorry: I wanted everything, children, husband, house, a family, and to write. Bumping along, improvising, however I could, but I managed it and sometimes, when I allow myself, I feel proud. Don't tell anyone). Unless otherwise noted, all translations of quotations are my own.

the novel narrates Igarzábal's experience as a writer, but that section also has its own author. Attributed to the fictional Evelynne Harrington, it is an ending that returns the reader to the beginning. To a beginning before writing—before memory, before words—but also to the beginning of Gorodischer's novel, the first section of which is attributed to the main character of the third. As Diana Battaglia points out, each narrator's authority is undermined if not negated by the narrator's status as fictional (140). Graciela Aletta de Sylvas stresses that "El texto constituye así un espacio de múltiples dimensiones en el que se confrontan diferentes escrituras, ninguna de las cuales es la original" (234; the text constitutes a multi-dimensional space in which different writings, none of which is the original, come face to face). Moreover, "aquí las distintas historias se articulan con independencia de una instancia central" (235; here the distinct stories are articulated independent of a central instance). No one of these stories is the definitive version; all are equally real. Karen Emmerich has written persuasively on the instability of the purported "original" that lies behind any translation, highlighting the translator's frequent role as editor as well as the multiple forms a text may take, among them consecutive editions, an author's revisions, and the transcription of script to type. In translating *Tumba de jaguares*, I have worked from the 2005 Emecé edition, the only edition of which I am aware, in consultation with the author. Yet the awareness of the receding or indeterminate source of a translation resonates with the reader's experience of this novel, which presents multiple origin stories for the central images without privileging any one of them as the definitive source.

Among Gorodischer's many novels, *Jaguars' Tomb* is the one that most directly addresses the abductions and disappearances that occurred under the military dictatorship of 1976–83. In an

interview published in 2006, Gorodischer describes speaking
of the dictatorship *al sesgo* (at a slant or obliquely) in *Jaguars'
Tomb* (Ferrero, *"Tumba"* 153). When Adrián Ferrero asks about
the choice to write about the Argentine Dirty War and state
terrorism from the perspective of a father whose daughter has
been taken, Gorodischer replies: "Necesitaba la presencia del
dolor y no debe haber dolor más grande que ése" (*"Tumba"*
153; I needed the presence of pain and there can't be any pain
greater than that). In an earlier interview she stated: "tenía la
impresión de que había que escribir algo sobre el horror de la
dictadura, cosa que yo no puedo hacer, porque lo encuentro
demasiado enorme. [. . .] Cuando encontré al escritor me di
cuenta—él me lo dijo—porqué estaba sufriendo tanto y porqué
no podía escribir" (quoted in Aletta de Sylvas 238–39; I had the
impression that I needed to write something about the horror
of the dictatorship, something I cannot do, because I find it too
vast. [. . .] When I found the writer I realized—he told me—why
he was suffering so and why he could not write). The character
told her why he was suffering, why he was blocked; the character's story is an attempt to approach, indirectly yet honestly,
the enormity of the horror.

   Part one, "Hidden Variables" ("Variables ocultas") by María
Celina Igarzábal, is narrated by Bruno Seguer. Seguer is the
author of the second part, "Recounting from Zero" ("Contar
desde zero") of which Evelynne Harrington, author of the
third, is a central character. Harrington, finally, is the author
of "Uncertainty" ("La incertidumbre") whose protagonist is
the dying Igarzábal. The three sections might suggest the time
of preparing to write, the novel written, and the moment of
looking back on a life of writing. Each of the three parts repeats
images from the others, in particular the octagonal room that is

in turn the jaguars' tomb, the central space of the torture center, the heart of an abandoned house that hides an adulterous affair. Each of the three partial novels circles that nearly round space and the loss that might be seen at its center: Seguer's loss of his daughter; the disappearance of Harrington's husband into the jungle; Igarzábal's loss of her husband and her husband's loss of his memory.

Bruno Seguer wants to write the story of a young woman from far away, but is frustrated by his inability to write past the insistent horror of his daughter's abduction and disappearance. "Hidden Variables," narrated by Seguer, traces his efforts to replace one set of mental images with those he would prefer to invent. The sentences are long and complex, often changing direction or describing different moments as if they overlapped. Seguer's monologue is left unfinished because the narrator is unable to continue, blocked by the painful repetition of his memories that are not quite memories, that stop, in imagination, just before the worst of the worst that must have happened. Seguer is troubled, too, by the difficulty of imagining what a woman—his invented character—feels, a character who is not (must not be) his daughter or his ex-wife, and yet whose experience is to some degree limited by what he knows, or believes he knows, about the women who have shared his life. Finally, Seguer is blocked, practically and metaphorically, because the author—his author—chose not to finish the book. The section ends, midsentence, with Seguer's apparent suicide. The final word of the section is "fin" or "end," which I have translated as "at last," because it appears in the phrase, "por fin." Yet that final phrase is unpunctuated—it is not finished with the full stop period of "the end," as if the word FIN floated alone at the bottom of the page.

"Recounting from Zero" is the novel Seguer wanted to write, the story of a young woman and the older man she travels to marry at his home in the land of the great rivers. She comes to hate her husband, who eventually disappears into the jungle; when he reappears, months later, the two achieve a prickly reconciliation. This section of Gorodischer's novel is divided into short, titled chapters, and the writing style is more spare than in the first part. The landscape is self-consciously "exotic," peopled by nomadic tribes and centered on the packing and shipment of an unspecified cargo down river. In this second part of the novel, Saccomanno finds a parallel with the tone and geography of Isak Dinesen's prose. Another literary echo might be Alejo Carpentier's *Los pasos perdidos*. Evelynne Harrington, who is never named in this section, occupies two worlds, that of her new home and that of the novel she wants to write, whose protagonist, Celina, is unaware that her supposedly dead husband did not in fact die when his plane crashed. The unpolished wooden table where Evelynne imagines herself writing (and where, in the third part, Celina writes), recalls Virginia Woolf's "room of one's own." Evelynne seeks distance from her prior life and from the daily violence crystalized in the bloodied face she sees in a tabloid newspaper and is unable to erase from her mind. Worse still is the assault on her sister Bridget, a harsh attack that strengthens Evelynne's resolve to put as much distance as possible between herself and the life she has known. That distance, she believes, will allow her to write. Although Evelynne has always been solitary, at a remove from her friends and family, the terror of her sister's assault, the silence and fear into which the family is plunged, the demand that she somehow be present—all of these contribute to Evelynne's decision to get away. She is unable to imagine her sister's fear, what she felt at the moment of attack, and although Bridget will get better, Evelynne will not stay to watch. The attack on her sister undermines Evelynne's sense of safety and robs her of her freedom to move through the world at will. By contrast, her husband's disappearance presents a degree of freedom, allowing her to take control of the next shipments and to approach the native tribes with the curiosity and respect that he had scorned. In his absence, she achieves a figurative sisterhood with the local women when she saves another woman's life, partially compensating for the emptiness left by her own sister's distance.

In "Uncertainty," the dying novelist María Celina Igarzábal recalls her own literary career (the titles of her books suggest a degree of popular best-sellerdom), an affair that ended in murder, and her husband's presumed death. This segment is again a single section, without chapter breaks, and is narrated in the third person. Cynthia Palmer discusses Gorodischer's treatment of older women as protagonists in two short stories from the collection *Menta,* concluding that Gorodischer achieves "an act of literary transfiguration by imagining old age as a dynamic site of creative possibility" (187). One of these stories, "Ars amandi," Palmer argues, offers a "sly parody of the edifying models of elder female empowerment found in many late-life fictions by women writers," and develops threads evident in Gorodischer's prior fiction (180). By contrast, Palmer suggests, in its focus on an old woman confined to a nursing home and marginalized, the story "Los que deciden la suerte del mundo" "marks a significant departure" (183). Published when Gorodischer was in her late seventies, *Jaguars' Tomb* might fairly be termed a "late-life fiction," though it is by no means Gorodischer's final word. The old woman represented in the novel, the novelist Celina Igarzábal, does not resort to crime (as does the protagonist of

"Ars amandi"); she endures the indignities of the nurses' endearments with a mixture of resignation and resistance. She spits out the doctor's little blue pills—a sedative meant to make her sleep—and uses the hospital solitude to look back on a life at times lonely, but also successful. She retains her interest in the details of her surroundings, always making connections to her past experiences or to her writing. The spider is a recurring image in this final section, with its resonances of weaving and textiles and of storytelling. The unfinished novel that is the first part of *Jaguars' Tomb* is mentioned explicitly. Its being unfinished is a source of some sadness for Celina, and again the figure is circular—her unfinished novel is about a man writing a novel that will remain unfinished.

The abduction of Bruno Seguer's daughter is the first traumatic absence to appear in the novel, but it is not the only one. That the disappearance of Chela-Chelita is one among many does not cheapen her death but rather reflects the extent to which the disappeared, although physically absent, remain present as a thread woven into the survivors' daily existence. Seguer's monologue is an indictment of the need to coexist with such an absence, to exist despite or after such a loss. In the course of the novel, one character uses Chela-Chelita's suffering and disappearance as a way to understand (express, deflect) her own sorrow; another uses someone else's suffering to avoid thinking about Chela-Chelita. One person's means is another person's end. One person's refuge is another person's trap—the jaguars' cave, refigured; the octagonal room. In addition to the preoccupation with loss and absence, the effort to write through and also about that emptiness, the three parts of Gorodischer's novel are linked through words and images, such as the piano, the octagonal room, and the city in the clouds.

For each of the writers in the novel, the relationship between experience and representation is layered. In the third part, Celina recalls finding herself unable to produce or imagine the right pain to address Bruno's experience. For Celina, so much time had passed since Ricardo's death that when she began to write "Hidden Variables," at first she felt no pain at all, nothing as deep as Seguer's sorrow. Initially, she planned to superimpose one over the other, her painful loss of Ricardo and Bruno's awareness that he will never recover his daughter's body. Yet she found the situations were too different: "ella no había perdido a nadie en los sótanos del horror y la vergüenza, y fue allí cuando resolvió finalmente que no, que en el caso de su personaje [. . .] el reflejo del dolor tendría que venir de otra parte" (181–82; she had not lost anyone in the cellars of horror and shame, and it was then that she finally concluded that no, in the case of her character [. . .] the reflection of that sorrow would have to come from somewhere else). The capacity to distance herself makes her wonder if she's heartless, able to make use of the greatest suffering —her own, or what she might have observed in others—only to "quedarse un frío instante en suspenso, intrigada pensando cómo puede poner eso en palabras" (182; remain for a cold instant in suspense, intrigued, thinking how she might put that into words). A part of her suffering, perhaps, is her awareness of her capacity to distance herself from that suffering in search of the appropriate words. Diana Battaglia prefaces her article on *Tumba de jaguares* with an epigraph taken from Gorodischer's *Historia de mi madre*, a book Battaglia describes as an "autobiographical novel" (137). The epigraph refers to words as a cushion, a protection or defense against harsh or frightening reality. Words—written words—never quite achieve that cushioning protection for these characters, but they hold out that promise.

As Osvaldo Aguirre observes, each of the three protagonists' reflections on writing center on the question of what it is possible to write, what purpose writing serves. Aguirre notes:

> Preguntarse cómo es posible escribir significa aquí hablar de lo que no se puede escribir. Y del sentido, de la pertinencia de escribir en mundos desgarrados por el dolor, la crueldad, el odio, el engaño. Los tres escritores de esta novela hablan sobre la imposibilidad de escribir y esta imposibilidad tiene que ver no con cuestiones técnicas o de falta de inspiración sino con una pérdida, con el modo en que la escritura se sitúa ante una pérdida. Y ante el revés de la pérdida, que es la espera: la espera de una hija desaparecida durante la dictadura militar, la espera de un marido ausente, la espera de la muerte.

> *To ask how it is possible to write here means to speak of what cannot be written. And of the significance, of the relevance of writing in worlds torn apart by pain, by cruelty, by hatred, by deceit. The three writers of this novel talk about the impossibility of writing and this impossibility has to do not with technical issues or lack of inspiration but rather with a loss, with the way in which writing is situated before a loss. And before the inverse of loss, which is waiting: waiting for a daughter disappeared during the military dictatorship, waiting for an absent husband, waiting for death.*

The importance of waiting is evident throughout the novel, coupled with varying degrees of impatience or resignation.

Although *Jaguars' Tomb* is made up of three distinct fragments, the three stories overlap or touch at numerous points; as Adrián Ferrero notes, the three stories are in fact components of a single tale ("*Tumba*" 150). Yet, Ferrero argues, the three voices remain distinct, reflecting ideologies that are distinct from, if not opposite to, one another; ultimately, writing "les permite como un hallazgo encontrar sentido en un universo entre cuyos signos parecen moverse con perplejidad, torpeza o debilidad" (*"Tumba"* 150; allows them to discover meaning in a universe amongst whose signs they seem to move with bewilderment, clumsiness, or weakness). Evelynne, as writer, wants to write about a woman whose husband survived the plane crash that apparently killed him. As character, Evelynne is the protagonist of a story in which, again, the husband's disappearance is only apparent. These apparent disappearances suggest an oblique resolution to Bruno Seguer's unanswerable grief. In Celina's case, although she does not know her husband survived, the reader can take some solace in the thought that at least he was happy elsewhere; for both of them, life goes on. In Evelynne's case, her husband's reappearance might respond to the fantasy of the bereaved for whom the loved one's loss never feels entirely real, entirely final—an unreality exacerbated, in the case of a person disappeared (or lost at sea, or in the jungle) by the absence of a body to recognize and mourn.

Seguer wants to write "something else," and tries to write something else, to save himself, to escape the painful repetitive memories, but he does not know if writing about a woman who escapes the fate his daughter did not will allow him to feel closer to his daughter, or if the necessary attention to how to say things—attention to the writing, to the words—will instead serve only to distance him further. For years, in interviews, he has claimed offhandedly that the alternate reality created in his fiction is indeed real. Now Seguer tries to push through the metaphorical to the concrete, to make the metaphor an embodied reality. Battaglia observes that the movement between existence and nonexistence among the various worlds of these stories undermines easy dichotomies: "Durante toda la narración hay una neta contaminación entre un nivel pretendido como 'real' y otro nivel asumido como 'ficcional' (141; Throughout the narrative there is a clear contamination between a level supposed to be "real" and another level accepted as "fictional"). The movement between realities, or versions of reality, approaches what Seguer (as a character who is also a writer) so desperately seeks: a reality that is other than the reality that surrounds him and that, crucially, is no less real.

Gorodischer's novel presents a puzzle, a textual game. Though a notion of "playful" carries a light tone, a game is not necessarily a lighthearted entertainment; play does not imply trivial pastime. As Pablo de Santis emphasizes, "La forma de la obra y su carácter lúdico (afín a Borges y a Calvino) choca con la dureza de las historias, como si el recurso de la ficción dentro de la ficción no tuviera por fin 'irrealizar' lo escrito sino, por el contrario, poner en escena el drama del escritor que inventa mundos mientras su propio mundo se 'desinventa' y se apaga" (The form of the work and its playful character [similar to Borges and to Calvino] clashes with the harshness of the stories, as if the device of the fiction within a fiction did not have the goal of making unreal what was written but rather, on the contrary, to put on stage the drama of the writer who invents worlds while his own world is "disinvented" and goes out). The narrator of the second and third parts does not intervene in the action, does not identify him or herself, but the perspective is largely limited to that of the protagonists, Evelynne Harrington in "Recounting from Zero," Celina Igarzábal in "Uncertainty." In each case the writer appears as a writer, considering what to write, how to write, where to write.

"Al sesgo"—Gorodischer's phrase recalls Emily Dickinson's poem, "tell all the truth but tell it slant," suggesting one possible guide for reading the novel:

> Tell all the truth but tell it slant –
> Success in Circuit lies
> Too bright for our infirm Delight
> The Truth's superb surprise
> As Lightning to the Children eased
> With explanation kind
> The Truth must dazzle gradually
> Or every man be blind –

Admittedly, I am drawn to the poem here by the first line, with its echoing of Gorodischer's phrasing. In Silvina Ocampo's translation:

> Toda la verdad decidla pero al sesgo –
> el éxito mora en rodeos
> demasiado brillante para nuestro doliente deleite
> la verdad soberbia sorprende
> como el relámpago a los niños
> que una buena explicación tranquiliza
> la verdad tiene que deslumbrar gradualmente
> o todo hombre será ciego –
> (1998, 67)

In the context of translation, and of visual approaches to the editing and interpreting of Dickinson's poetry, Karen Emmerich discusses distinct versions of this poem at some length (see her chapter 3, "On Manuscripts, Type-Translation, and Translation

(Im?)proper: Emily Dickinson and the Translation of Scriptural Form"). The edition of Ocampo's translations cited here contains no editorial apparatus or evident intervention beyond a brief biographical note opposite the title page. The poems appear unnumbered, without index, and the source edition or editions are not identified. Ocampo's translation is copyright 1985, prior to the variorum editions of Dickinson's work published in the 1990s, much less the online, open-access *Emily Dickinson Archive*.

Several points might be remarked on in this Spanish version. The choice of the *vosotros* form of the second-person imperative —*decid*—reflects a usage more Peninsular than Argentine, but also the fact that the English imperative is more ambiguous; the subject of the imperative may be plural or singular, formally or informally addressed. Ocampo breaks the poem into two four-line stanzas, and makes choices with syntax that clarify some points while muddying others. The phrase "la verdad soberbia sorprende" seems to imply that truth is surprising pride or arrogance, though *soberbia* may mean magnificence as well. Ocampo's second stanza is more prosaic, more straightforwardly explanatory; her first stanza is more musical, with its pairings "doliente deleite" and "soberbia sorprende." As a point of entry into *Jaguars' Tomb* and the writing processes of the three protagonists, Ocampo's translation retains the important sense of a gradual bedazzlement, an approach that might make the truth not only visible, but able to be seen.

In an essay titled "Tell it Slant," Camille Dungy takes Dickinson's poem as a starting point to "think more critically about how poets introduce fundamental truths in ways readers can carry with them, ways that won't be so alarming that a reader will refuse to accept the poem's vision of the world." Discussing poems that, as she puts it, engage in "direct telling circuitously," Dungy stresses that "To be oblique is not the same as to be opaque. Obliqueness refers to angles and slopes, to geometry that is not parallel." The octagonal room, an image that recurs throughout the novel, described as being "so octagonal it was almost round," hints at a geometry of curves and angles combined, in which *octagonal* is a matter of degree, not definition.

So octagonal, it was almost round—that is, it is always very nearly something else. In each of the sections of the novel, the room represents a transitional space, an anteroom. Graciela Aletta de Sylvas highlights the shifts or transformations in the room "so octagonal it was almost round," from the torture chamber to the setting of a developing romance, from death to love (240–41). In the third part of the novel, the octagonal room is both the setting for illicit romance and hidden sex, and a scene of murder. Celina recalls that she had experienced "una vida secreta, estremecedora, en la habitación casi redonda de tan octagonal, esa habitación que era como una araña con sus ocho patas cada una en una pared" (193; a secret, heart-rending life in the room so octagonal it was almost round, that room that was like a spider with its eight legs, each one on a wall). She imagines the room filled with voices, with gestures, a tangible memory of those who have occupied the room before her, in happiness or agony. The octagonal room is the final space Celina enters, the culmination of the images and memories she traces, connects and disconnects, "el paisaje que la va rodeando, combándose a su alrededor hasta formar un almenar casi redondo de tan octagonal, puro fulgor, sólo paredes" (217; the landscape that is surrounding her, bending around her until it forms a crenellation almost round, it's so octagonal, pure brilliance, only walls).

Jaguars' Tomb is a widely allusive novel, drawing in references to Shakespeare, Somerset Maugham, Gustavo Adolfo Bécquer, Jorge Luis Borges, and others. Some allusions are direct, others are more oblique. For instance, lines from Bécquer's "Rima VII" ("del salón en el ángulo oscuro, de su dueña tal vez olvidada") are quietly incorporated, without attribution, into Celina's recollection of childhood visits with her cousin Myrtha-with-a-y-after-the-M. More overtly, Mrs. Albert Forrester, protagonist of Maugham's story "The Creative Impulse," is explicitly invoked when Celina's husband Ricardo recalls his life on the sidelines of her literary career. Ricardo is tired of so much literature, so much art—"cansado de tanta literatura, tanto arte" (176); his thinking echoes Albert Forrester's farewell note: "I have had all the literature I can stand and I am fed up with art" (Maugham 422). More obliquely, the repeated references to jaguars might recall Jorge Luis Borges' story "The Writing of the God" as well as the importance of the jaguar in Mesoamerican mythologies. Aletta de Sylvas discusses the significance of the jaguar in pre-Columbian Mayan and Aztec mythologies, and underscores the role of the jaguars in destroying the first creation (237). Battaglia highlights a further resonance of the jaguar, finding an echo of Borges' story. She writes, "Como lectores memoriosos, el texto de Gorodischer evocó en nosotros a otro jaguar, compañero de cautiverio de aquel prisionero azteca que trata de descifrar en los dibujos de sus manchas el sentido del universo o sea la escritura de Dios" (142; as readers with a good memory, Gorodischer's text evoked for us another jaguar, companion in captivity of that Aztec prisoner who tries to decipher, in the designs of its spots, the meaning of the universe or rather the writing of God). In Borges' story, the prisoner shares his prison with a jaguar, "que mide con secretos pasos iguales el tiempo y el espacio del cautiverio" (Borges, "La escritura" 117; "which with secret, unvarying paces measures the time and space of its captivity" [Borges, "The Writing" 250]). Aguirre suggests that the image of the jaguars' tomb represents "algo que quizá no podrá ser dicho, o que no alcanzará una expresión definitiva, pero que en cada acercamiento deja marcas para no ser olvidado" (something that perhaps will not be able to be said, or that will not reach a definitive expression, but that in every approach leaves marks so as not to be forgotten). The narrator of Borges' story, seemingly condemned to eternal life within that cave, recalls the tradition of a perfect sentence written by the god that might conjure the end of the world, a sentence that in its perfection unwrites the speaker, erases the speaking self.

Gorodischer's novel is rich in repetitions, both within and between sections, of sounds, words, and phrases. Plays on similarity of sound or meaning (for example, a language of "sílabas silbadas," whistled syllables) are common, as are plays on words with multiple meanings, such as the verb *contar*, meaning both to tell and to count. The title of the second part, "Contar desde zero" became "Recounting from Zero" in an effort to carry both of those meanings forward.

Bruno Seguer describes his difficulty writing as well as the novel he wants to be writing, about a young woman from a northerly, foggy country who is also writing a novel. Although conventionally, one of the chief characteristics of dialogue on the page is that it is marked as such, with some kind of attribution expected (they said, we said), here remembered dialogue with his ex-wife Gabriela, his daughter's mother, is embedded in Seguer's narrative. The character's fumbling after what he wants to say, and the obsessive repetition of his memories as he tries to write, are significant; the thread should not be *too* easy to follow. In Seguer's recollection:

La novela le sirve como al hombre de los grandes ríos el trabajo, y a mí me sirve la novela de ella y la de él como trabajo que me aísla del mundo en el que suceden cosas inimaginables, fuera de todos los límites en los que se mueve lo que es humano. Y entonces cuando Gabriela viene y me dice ¿y vos qué? vos, que te quedás encerrado llorando; trabajando, corrijo yo; llorando, insiste ella; vos, en vez de venir y hacerte oír con nosotras; por eso yo le digo que nadie las va a oír, nunca, y que es mejor hacer lo que yo hago, hacer algo, transformar lo que es dado en lo que nunca será" (Gorodischer, *Tumba de jaguares* 21).

The novel serves her the way work serves the man of the great rivers, and the way her novel and his serve me as work that separates me from the world where unimaginable things happen, things beyond the limits within which all that is human moves. And then when Gabriela comes and says to me, and what about you? you, who stay inside crying; working, I correct; crying, she insists; you, instead of coming out and making yourself heard with us; so I tell her no one is going to hear those women, ever, and it is better to do what I do, make something, transform what is given into what will never be.

Nosotras in the Spanish is an implicit reference to the Mothers of the Plaza de Mayo, as they demand the return of their children who were disappeared. English has no similarly gendered first person plural. In the translation, I opted to insert "those women" for the more general—but still feminine—"las," which might otherwise have been rendered as "them." That the group Gabriela wanted Seguer to join is a group of women is important.

Translation is mentioned and incorporated within the novel. As Celina begins to find success, she earns prestige and sometimes money—particularly, it is stressed, when her books are translated into other languages. Her lost husband Ricardo, amused that his English doctor bears the name of a French writer (André Maurois), adopts the name Johnny Keats in place of the one he has forgotten. Evelynne, a student of languages, applies herself to learning the languages of the several tribes whose members work at La Preciada.

Translations of well-known texts are also embedded in the novel. Seguer reads *A Midsummer Night's Dream* with his daughter, an activity the two enjoy so much that they create their own version, throwing in everything they can think of from their own imaginations. When they move on to the poems, a Spanish translation of Shakespeare's Sonnet 116 is woven seamlessly into Seguer's internal monologue, marked only by a capital letter distinguishing the first word:

A él le gustaría nuestra versión de su sueño, decía yo, quién es él decía ella, Shakespeare decía yo, un muchacho que escribía teatro y poemas, leamos los poemas decía ella y yo le recitaba No me opongo a que se unan almas leales pero amor no es amor si mal templado cambia si encuentra cambios eventuales y es al olvido dócil inclinado, y ella lo aprendía de memoria y me lo recitaba ella a mí, con ademanes, decía, como se lo enseñaban en la escuela, con ademanes. (Gorodischer, Tumba de jaguares 26)

He would like our version of his dream, I said, who is he, she said, Shakespeare, I said, a guy who wrote plays and poems, let's read the poems, she said and I recited for her Let me not to the marriage of true minds admit impediment love is not love which alters when it alteration finds or bends with the remover to remove and she learned it from memory and recited it to me, with gestures, she said, the way they taught in school, with gestures.

Shakespeare's lines will likely be at least vaguely familiar for most readers. If not, the relevant parts of the poem have been included. The emphasis on gestures, expressions—another of the novel's many repetitions—and the idea of remembered, repeated performance or enactment are the most important elements here, along with the understanding that each reenactment or recitation draws on a long history of prior texts, events, recollections, and illusions. In translating this section, I did not back-translate from the Spanish, but inserted the lines from Shakespeare's sonnet directly. The sonnet's role here is to provide recognizable and reciteable language, to convey a shareable tradition, not to delve into semantic subtleties. A text like *Jaguars' Tomb*, with its overlapping and incomplete cross-references, invites an associative reading; all the more so in the case of translation of the novel. A translation is a recontextualized reading. With respect to the source text, it is inescapably out of context. Yet a translation generates a new, different reading context, one conditioned by the translator's choices and by the circumstances of the reader.

Jaguars' Tomb is one book told in many voices, a microcosm, taken as a whole, of a writer's work—recycling, refashioning, attempting to describe or imagine experience and then put it into words, again and again. The final internal monologue of *Jaguars' Tomb* is a transfiguration, an ending that is made into something new or possible without undue hope or easy resolution. Celina, too, has "told it slant": "No había escrito sobre sus padres o sus hermanos o las casas en las que había vivido [. . .] y especialmente sobre la tarea de escribir. No había escrito la muerte de Ricardo ni la habitación casi redonda de tan octagonal. [. . .] También es cierto que había escrito sobre todo eso sólo que sin nombrarlo" (158; She had not written about her parents or her brothers or the houses she had lived in [. . .] and especially about the task of writing. She had not written about Ricardo's death or the room so octagonal it was almost round. [. . .] It is also true that she had written about all of that, only without naming it). The "truths" of the *Jaguars' Tomb* have not been made palatable, and the central absence of each narrative remains an emptiness. The circular structure of the novel retains this emptiness, protects it, frustrating the reader's attempt to resolve the stories' contradictions even as it presents the opening—the invitation—of that ending that is in fact a return to the beginning.

WORKS CITED

Aguirre, Osvaldo. "Ficción vertiginosa." *La Capital* (Rosario, Argentina). 23 October 2005. http://archivo.lacapital.com.ar/2005/10/23/seniales/noticia_239333.shtml.

Aletta de Sylvas, Graciela. *La aventura de escribir: La narrativa de Angélica Gorodischer.* Corregidor, 2009.

Battaglia, Diana. "La narración en su laberinto: Análisis de *Tumba de jaguares* de Angélica Gorodischer." *Creación y proyección de los discursos narrativos.* Ed. Daniel Altamiranda and Esther Smith. Dunken, 2008. 137–44.

Borges, Jorge Luis. "La escritura del dios." *El Aleph.* Alianza/Emecé, 1971. 117–23.

——. "The Writing of the God." *Collected Fictions.* Trans. Andrew Hurley. Viking, 1998. 250–54.

de Santis, Pablo. "Lazos de escritura." *La Nación.* 9 October 2005. http://www.lanacion.com.ar/745770-lazos-de-escritura.

Dickinson, Emily. *The Poems of Emily Dickinson: Reading Edition.* Ed. Ralph W. Franklin. Belknap Press of Harvard University Press, 1998.

Dungy, Camille T. "Tell It Slant: How to Write a Wise Poem." Poetry Foundation. 10 June 2014. https://www.poetryfoundation.org/articles/70128/tell-it-slant.

Emmerich, Karen. *Literary Translation and the Making of Originals.*
   Bloomsbury, 2017.

Ferrero, Adrián, and Angélica Gorodischer. *"Tumba de jaguares." Chasqui* 35.1
   (2006): 148–53.

————. "Entrevista." *Hispamérica* 43.127 (April 2014): 33–39.

Gorodischer, Angélica. *Tumba de jaguares.* Emecé, 2005.

Maugham, W. Somerset. "The Creative Impulse." *The Complete Short Stories
   of W. Somerset Maugham.* Doubleday, 1953. 403–36. Vol. 1 of *East and West.*

Ocampo, Silvina, trans. *Emily Dickinson: 60 poemas.* By Emily Dickinson.
   Mondadori, 1998.

Palmer, Cynthia L. "Rupture and Rebellion: Reimagining the Older Woman
   in Two Short Stories by Angélica Gorodischer." *Romance Notes* 47.2
   (2007): 179–88.

Saccomanno, Guillermo. "Los '70 de Gorodischer." *Página12 (Radar Libros).*
   25 September 2005. https://www.pagina12.com.ar/diario/suplementos/
   libros/10-1755-2005-09-25.html.

JAGUARS' TOMB

El azar se diluye en la dulce indiferencia del mundo.
IVAR EKELAND

HIDDEN
VARIABLES

———

María Celina Igarzábal

VANDERBILT UNIVERSITY PRESS
Nashville, Tennessee

Anything can be everything
and each is also its opposite.

ROBERT KAPLAN

I DREAMT I WAS IN HEAVEN. Not Heaven, paradise of fortunate souls. In the heavens, that sky blue—what? elytron?—that officially covers all of us, covers religions that promise eternal happiness as much as it does wretched poems, clumsily rhymed. In the heavens, up there above where, a poor imitation, a mirror of our own, there's another city. Standing on dense clouds, hard as bitumen, compact, immobile as stone angels, clouds sprawled like sacks of corn, I felt no fear that I might fall and fall and smash against the ground. I think it fair to say I felt nothing. Indifference, maybe; or something still more disagreeable, like boredom. Poor heavens, to harbor this ill-humored man, even if it was but to show him the other side of the clouds, just for a moment. So much, so little, so miserly—I thought I should give something in exchange, that I was expected to give something, but what? What more can I give after giving what I gave, what they tore from me? I only know how to write, but words are little if it's payment—although it could also be a debt—if it's a matter of payment, of price. Or maybe I could sing, recount in a reverse accounting all the anguish and we're back to the matter of the words. Poor heavens.

Lying on a high bed of clouds, I looked around and saw the city. Not the city down below, the city in the clouds. It was a city—it could have been any of them, or none, it made no difference; a city, yes, that's what it was, one of the largest. It was enormous, flooded with skyscrapers as if that were a way to defend it, to make it appear (or even be) invulnerable, and it was. I turned on my side so as to see it better and then I saw it the way it had to be seen: static, deserted, all white, the buildings perforated by tiny windows. I didn't see gardens, or monuments or balconies or inhabitants or libraries or streets or bars or schools; only the city, the buildings that were the city; and the more I looked, the more solid and unfortunate it seemed. I thought it must be infinite, because one always returns to that which is probably infinite, desolate before the mystery and sheltered by its grandeur. That's what gave it the contagious air of distress. Or maybe, it occurred to me on waking—because even as I was confirming my uneasiness, I woke up—maybe it had been built by the misfortune of a dying people who, knowing they were dying, left a monument. In the heavens, not in Heaven.

Up there, perhaps, there would be no storms and the sun would always be shining on the high towers, perforated and still.

No storms. Not sandstorms nor rainstorms nor snowstorms; storms like the ones I imagine on the riverbank at La Preciada, beyond the big curve, the whole place exposed to the west winds that carry dust and sand, and little men running to cover the canoes and tie up the animals; storms that form in five minutes and last at most an hour, an hour and a half, unless they let loose in the middle of the night, crossing the darkness to clear up in the morning over sleeplessness and mud.

But that is not—no, no, it isn't—that is not the best way to start to tell the story, so as to tell, first of all, about what happened or should have happened. The storms at La Preciada are something she encounters; they are not—not yet—part of her own story. It is his story, it has been for years, many years—long enough to feel the weight is growing too heavy for him.

Her story begins much earlier and much further north. Let's see. A different beginning, different words, what is necessary but not too much; what begins to slip, not shame but maybe—just barely—a lie.

Or if not that, why not begin with the man who, being tired, dreams of a city in the heavens?

No, no, no, it really is not necessary, it is not even desirable, to get into something from over there when it just now happened to me, to this person, this writer: I, me, Bruno Seguer, the author who is not supposed to appear on the same stage as the storms. What happens doesn't happen to the author, it shouldn't happen to him; what happens, happens to the people of La Preciada, to the girl from the cold country of fog, to the plainsmen and to the man who longs for a piano.

It is a novel, not a diary or a confession, not an outpouring of sentiment. He doesn't dream about anything. He is simply tired. He has lived and worked in that house beside that river for years. Perhaps he needs to change. Not to leave, move the business, build another jetty. He has thought, at times—but isn't it out of place, this making the rounds of his plans?—thought at times about bringing a woman to live with him, but he couldn't endure a native, and as for white women out there, don't even mention it. The native women are fine for a few hours or a few days, not to live with. If there were one here in the house day and night, what would she do? What would she do? Embroider? Help Tuca bake the bread? Learn to read? And what would he do, what would he say to her? How could he look at that passive and distant face, maybe with shiny paint on cheeks and forehead, a headband hung with the fangs of brown desert rats if he allowed it? No.

It isn't that. He doesn't want women living in the house, nor (probably) does he want to change his life. He asks himself often, he asks himself but he doesn't know nor does it seem he wants to answer, if what he wants is to go back. But it's neither one nor the other—nor, he wants to believe, does he wish his life had been different.

And I, in spite of these doubts, faced with him (and without telling him or telling myself), I know exactly what he feels and how he feels it, but the same doesn't happen with her. It even seems hopeless. I can't imagine what a woman feels who both hates and desires the man who desires her, or who in any case desires that man who is capable of hatred and who desires a woman, any woman.

I do not know, but it is not hopeless. I can make do, precisely because I do know—to know is not to feel—I do know where the words are, where I have to look for them, even though I might be unable to reach them; the words to say what I don't feel but imagine, the way he imagines the woman who is imagining him while she writes the letter. Maybe it is, how to say it, my experience, that part of my life with women—so few, everything so limited by pain, by distance, by what one wants to forget and cannot. Those women, the same ones I don't want to think about, I don't want to. Only write. Before, before all of this, what did I write for? And now everything is so different and that woman shows up in writing and I can't protect her, either.

I tend to think of her as if she were a fool, but only because I can't imagine what she feels. With him, it's different, I know for certain. The self-assurance, the hardness, even if it is built up through an effort of disguise—whatever it is, he's much clearer. I know she buys a newspaper; for now, that's all I know.

And nonetheless, that isn't all. There is something of the places (it could not be otherwise) and there is that silent mob; no, not silent, simply incomprehensible, because it does not speak English or German or French or Spanish or Italian or anything approaching any of those languages of whose existence one is at least aware; these are not guttural but, say, marked, high accents, almost whistled syllables pulled outward from the palate and suddenly the knowing smile when she recognizes that there is no response to so much effort. So there is this much that I know and that they will come to know, little by little. And I think I know the ending and how it began.

Do I have to make myself a summary, a diagram, scattered notes, something to stand on? Or is that enough, vague as it is, so vague it sometimes seems unreachable? It began with a dream, a recurrent dream, the worst of dreams, cursed, unwanted, the bodies at the bottom of the trap, the dark, damp pit where they suffered, dying little by little. I know the title and I know why it's called *Recounting from Zero*, it's called that because there is no other option, because everything starts suddenly, from zero, from the most unbearable zero because it is not an emptiness, it is not the longed-for nothingness.

What I do not know, what I still do not know, what is not yet known, is how to put into words all that has been imagined. See? That's why one needs the plans and the summaries and the reflections in writing about what is to be written. Sometimes it all just comes along with its words, those words that belong to it, those that are necessary and not others, and that is a blessing. That's when what has been imagined is already in words; the obstacle lies elsewhere. But I can't make plans. I go looking and looking for that obstacle so as to pass over it or go around it, overcome it or circle it and then, yes, enter the seductive realm of words. And I know point by point what happens between that woman and that man—though it doesn't matter if it happens or not, because what is important is that I have been able to imagine it and therefore can also betray it. All that has been imagined exists, even if you wish it didn't, I tell myself. And because I know I am treading on dangerous ground, I go and, what do I do? I grab hold of the novel, celebrate the beginning so as not to return, repeat, fall into the pain I also imagine, "there must come a time to do something with that life, her life." Do something with that, with what's outside of life or at least outside this life I'm living, okay? Not the other that I have not lived, which is much worse—much worse—than this one. What happens is one goes back to one's own sores, those glued to one's flesh, to lick at them again and again in search of relief, or healing, or even looking for the pain, over and over the pain because finally it is not that there is one life over here and another, whoever's it might be (I don't want to think about whose, I don't want to), another over there, but rather that all lives, not leaving out even one, all of them are superimposed, confused, tangled, inextricably mixed—what a word, never use it, one should never use that type of word, never even if they throw themselves at you; and if possible, never adverbs, I hate adverbs—all lives, although you neither know it nor want them to be, all of them are combined in a mixture that is also physical, even if we don't realize it (most of all if we don't realize it) and we continue, we keep on going forward without wanting to believe that it is precisely (another adverb to be avoided and I have to go back over the text to see if I find it so I can erase it, use a phrase, open up the concept so as not to drop it there like an undesirable blemish), believe it is not the prudent or the expected thing or good sense but rather the unbelievable which propels us through the fog.

Fog of that country of the north that a girl thinks about at the beginning of her life, which is the beginning of the novel so that I can flee from the girls who now never, but never, will think about what their lives will be.

See if the other novel can be inserted, the one the girl writes while she's going through all that about the great rivers and the thing with her sister and death and the trap for wild beasts and waking up in the night to think about herself (only this time straight ahead, without going into pretexts) and about how she wants to be alone all her life, that foolishness . . . but in that case, careful, because for sure someone is going to bring up Chinese boxes and if there's one thing that ticks me off, it's that garbage about the Chinese boxes, poverty of language, lazy thinking, and besides, who even knows what Chinese boxes are, who has even seen Chinese boxes? Give me a break. For that reason, only talk about that novel, the one she writes, and how it serves her to, I don't know, maybe endure the transplant she has suffered—and sought, she sought it out, clearly—or to defend herself like she did at school or when she fled down the corridors of other languages that were not her own.

The novel serves her the way work serves the man of the great rivers, and the way her novel and his serve me as work that separates me from the world where unimaginable things happen, things beyond the limits within which all that is human moves. And then when Gabriela comes and says to me, and what about you? you, who stay inside crying; working, I correct; crying, she insists; you, instead of coming out and making yourself heard with us; so I tell her no one is going to hear those women, ever, and it is better to do what I do, make something, transform what is given into what will never be, but one day she came closer than others and she told me, "each one chooses the way to wriggle out so as not to feel the blade."

And I work, and when, like now, I can't and I can't, I know I have to write and I can't—

I look out the window and I ask myself, let's see, looking at the city in the clouds, why is it that I can't? Nothing occurs to me, I can't take the next step, although I know what comes next. And yesterday I said to myself—although I think it was today, very early—that the problem is I want everyone to be happy, everyone, including the girl from the cold north and the German man in the land of the great rivers, or especially those two, and beyond them everyone in all of those mixed up lives that remain each one itself and yet together make up a single whole. To put that into words—not the happiness, I mean, but what awaits them that is not happiness. As if I see them, I know they are there and that they have died, the two of them, in the treacherous pit, the jaguars' tomb, perhaps embracing or only touching, having gone through heaven and hell. But what I can't do is make them go through heaven and hell because I, I myself, although I have never been in heaven and only once in dreams in the city in the clouds, I live in this hell to which I try to give words that speak of that other hell, not mine, which—as with the lives—is that of everyone, is hers, is mine, is that of lives unknown. One step, a single step through that hell contaminates all the lives of each and every one and transforms them into this. This, which is like tracing a parapet walk, the rim of a wall, perhaps, surrounded by nothing, by a dark and nameless abyss into which one is always on the point of falling. One falls, sometimes one falls, but the terrible thing is not that death awaits below, in a torrent or a desert or a wilderness of rocks, but that what awaits one is to survive and to find oneself once again up on top and to continue walking along the narrow edge surrounded entirely by black. Black like the cells. I don't want to think, I want to keep writing, so maybe it would be better to abandon *Recounting from Zero* and begin something else—I have no idea at this moment what that something is—something which could come into being, which isn't here now but surely would present itself at the moment I called, the instant at which I empty myself of everything, words, memories, dreams, the music of a piano, the cursed geography of today's scorched walls that I wouldn't see when Gabriela came to put me up against the ropes ("even if it's only for this, which is an ending," she said), the smell, the smells I should say, the smell of suffering and of death, the smell of waiting in the night, that smell that clings to places people have passed through, traitorous smells, there to say what we do not want to hear; the others, those of happy summers, the distinctive smells of cities (everyone knows, Rio smells of alcohol, Barcelona of tobacco, Paris of coffee, Buenos Aires of stagnant grime, each one of them enclosed, as if the others did not exist); in that moment, when one feels nothingness is all there is around one, the blessed goad arrives, the bad light and behind it, as if a door had opened, a hole in the world of beings and things and empty skies, behind the carcass to which life must be returned: that's it, I tell myself, the task of the writer, and to that I dedicate my days and hopefully Gabriela will never, ever think to return, although I know she is going to call me on the telephone, she is going to leave messages ("of conscience," she calls them) on my answering machine; I hope she disappears, that she dies, that she goes to live in another country, that she is left paralyzed and mute forever; I hope she never again rings the bell and I don't have to open the door and see her, I don't want to see her, I want to erase her from my life, her hair pulled back and those hard eyes shoes with little golden buckles tailored suit the purse slung across her chest as if it were a cartridge belt and something in her hand, she always has something in her hand, the bag from the supermarket or a package or files or her glasses or a newspaper, something, as if it were the weapon she has to load and load against me to oblige me, that's her aim, to go out on the street with her and I have already told her no, my only weapon is this, it is words but written words, not those unspoken words of hers. No. Things must be said, I tell her, but she doesn't understand, she says she says them, that words are not just to construct novels, that's what she says, construct novels. And she truly doesn't say the words, and it's not a question of now but of before, of long before—I'd say always, but that isn't true. I don't know since when. Maybe ever since we separated, ever since Chela-Chelita began to grow up, stopped being a little girl and the two of us found ourselves faced with someone who was becoming unfathomable. I will never stop thinking Gabriela was to blame, she should have known or at least suspected something strange was going on. I don't hold myself blameless: no one is innocent, not I nor anybody else, but neither is it true that I was the absent one absorbed in my imagery like she said and that's why the girl looked elsewhere for support and belonging. Fine, that's just fine, very pretty but it isn't true. I was there, she was the one who prevented me from being there more, because she had English, she didn't feel well, there's a birthday party, she already left, she's studying, she has to help take the summer clothing out of the upper cupboard and put away the winter things, or her friends or math or the movies or the library or whatever it might be so as to, I suppose, not feel I was stealing her away, those are also her words and it is also untrue. If I had known. But thinking like that is less than worthless. I wanted to know, I always wanted to know, to find out as we went along because she was changing from one day to the next, like little puppies do, and I wasn't there at her side on all of those days, or from one to the next or for the minutes, the segments of her life. I wanted, I remember, to take her with me to Montevideo that year, what year, it's been so many years now, so many I don't remember, when there was the symposium on Latin American literature and she was happy, how she laughed, we're going to take advantage of our chance and go to the beach, I told her, we're going to take a boat ride, we're going to do everything by water, did you know there were hydroplanes once? And she didn't know what hydroplanes were just as she had never seen a streetcar or the Di Tella nor had she ever heard Juliette Greco, and I told her, I told her everything, all of that. Of course Gabriela couldn't stand our conversations, that's why she didn't let her go. She told me I put things in her head, strange things, she said. I did? I put things in her head? Gabriela was always like that, very limited, literal, concrete, this is how things are, everything has a cause, everything has a predictable result, there is no such thing as mystery, or the incomprehensible, that which is difficult if not impossible to know, to undertake so as to understand. She doesn't know that the things that do not exist help us to live, that the impossible is what ties us to life and when those things are no more, we die. She would never understand. But it's fine she's that way. That's all very well when one is a public accountant like she is and has an important position in an important company, but not if one wants to write (unless one has enough power to separate the two lives, something I never had) and I wanted Chela-Chelita to be like me, not a writer exactly but maybe, for example, an actress. If one wants to write, one has to live every instant, all of the instants, immersed in what one does not understand, precisely—that's it—precisely so as to write and thus see if that way one does understand, and yet to know that will never happen, but to go on, go on. An actress, too, moving and speaking up there as if nothing else existed and in spite of the lights immersed, she too, in shadow so as to give it life and color and voice, above all voice; for that reason I did what I could, maybe that was what she wanted or was going to want someday, and I told her about the life of Sarah Bernhardt and we watched Greta Garbo films she said were boring, she even said *Ninotchka* was boring and I told her when you're older you're going to understand and she said it takes a long time to grow up and she never did and she didn't like Liv Ullman so I resigned myself to not watching Bergman with her but I didn't give up showing her that everything in this world is many things at the same time, telling her that mathematics is all very well and getting a perfect 10 in math is even better but without passion mathematics wouldn't be possible, nor anything else; without madness, without disobedience, without curiosity, there is nothing. Yes there is, she said, and I recognized Gabriela's voice

and I set myself to erase it. *A Midsummer Night's Dream*, I suggested, let's read *A Midsummer Night's Dream* and that she did
like and we read it and each one played a part or two or three,
and since we added from our own store everything we could
think of, we ended up laughing at the crazy things we said. He
would like our version of his dream, I said, who is he, she said,
Shakespeare, I said, a guy who wrote plays and poems, let's
read the poems, she said and I recited for her Let me not to the
marriage of true minds admit impediment love is not love which
alters when it alteration finds or bends with the remover to
remove and she learned it from memory and recited it to me,
with gestures, she said, the way they taught in school, with
gestures; and so as to humor me, to see me happy, she said yes,
she wanted to be an actress, get up on the stages of the world
and play Phaedra—I don't know if she would have said that,
play Phaedra, maybe she did, I want to believe she did even
though what it was, what she said, what was said between the
two of us has become mist, a vague halo from which expressions sometimes emerge, the gestures of Chela-Chelita reciting
Shakespeare, sunshine that reaches us on the coastal promenade,
a coffee for me and a coca cola for her with a sandwich and
laughter and The Police and take me with you to Córdoba and
your mother doesn't want me to and try to arrange it and say
your mother knows what's best for you and missing a week of
school isn't good and her sulking until she got over it and once
again the laughter and I bought her a sky blue necklace. Where
is the necklace? I asked Gabriela during one of those awful
nights full of silence and of trying not to look at one another
face to face, the two of us next to the telephone waiting for a
call from I no longer even know whom that would tell us I no
longer know what. It never came, ever, not that nor any other

call. What necklace? she said. The blue necklace, the one with the little beads, the one with a clasp that always gives her trouble, I said, speaking in the present tense like a spell, like I was blackmailing destiny. I think she told me she was wearing it. I only think so. Although I don't want to think so, because the fact of her wearing it is so brutal, so monstrous, so unbearable that I may have forged it myself as a reconstruction of all my pain, an attempt to place it all there, in the necklace around her neck so as not to have to retrace over and over again the path of the wounds. Then I find I did not know, could not describe correctly what the English girl feels, apart from the fact that she is a she and she not only isn't me, but she's a woman and I will never be able to reach, out of incapacity or out of fear, what she feels when she knows or believes she knows that he has died in a horrible way—where?—and when she believes she will never know with certainty anything about his death, he who is no longer there, who will not return, she believes. Besides, it's not the same, it is not the same, how could it be? I can go back over the novel and change all that; I'm not able (or yes, I am, but I resist and I fail over and over again), I am not able to go back over the sky blue necklace around her neck and feel myself shatter as on other nights, at other moments, black days, always without consolation, without restraint, without hope, without the possibility of changing anything because everything has remained there in absence—and, worse, in what I can imagine as I imagine the night, above all the night, yes, it was night and she wore the necklace of sky blue beads around her neck because she had just come in from the street. From where? I asked Gabriela when she called me. What do I know, she yelled at me, what do I know? She didn't tell me anything, it's a long time since she told me anything, of course, what do you know if you only see her once in a while, and she went on and on that way and I felt the temptation to tell her fine but it's because you're stingy with her, you try to let me see her as little as possible. I didn't say it and she kept yelling and I held the receiver further away until I couldn't hear anything more than a kind of whistle that rose and fell and when it calmed down to a sob gave me time to tell her we could do something, surely, while panic rose up from my heels through my legs, weakening my knees, and from there to my waist through my back until it lodged at the nape of my neck like a heavy tumor that radiated not exactly pain but suspicion, the certainty that the pain was going to burst in the next second, it was going to flood my head and my life and my arms and ever afterward all the words that I could always and never speak or write. Calm down, I told her, I'm on my way over.

That was the first time, the one I remember most clearly, because after that the tumor grew and infected my entire life and I could no longer deny it my body and I began this practice of a perception blighted by everything that happened to her. I couldn't tell a story: Gabriela took care of that, of that and of the useless pilgrimages from which she returned utterly destroyed, from her flesh inward, and on which I once or twice accompanied her until I realized it was all useless. Not Gabriela, lucky for her, maybe—though it's hard to speak of luck since they took Chela-Chelita, and I don't know if hers might not be a misfortune even greater than mine. As for myself, nothing, except to continue living in this that cannot even be named. If it doesn't have a name, it doesn't exist, I tell myself. If you cannot attach words to it, say desperation, agony, the end of everything, if it is impossible to construct it as Gabriela says you do with your novels, then you are lost: without a name, that which does not exist because it does not have a word, that of which no one has experience or memory, that which is like death, that which is worse than death, gains on you and tears you apart over and over again and it bleeds you and it bites you and everything is useless because she is not there, Chela-Chelita is not going to come back, no one is going to bring her to me by the hand and tell me here she is, it was all a prank. I know this is not hopelessness, it is not the opposite of what Gabriela practices, but I suspect she also no longer hopes for anything, she only goes and goes again and asks and walks and protests and stands up and when she can no longer stand herself she looks for me and she hounds me so as to force me, as she puts it, to come out of myself, to come out of that empty world, to go, even if only to look at the ruins. I don't want to see that, I told her, and I didn't go. She says that way, seeing something concrete, terrible as it might be, that way one is certain everything has ended and it is possible, she says it's possible, to begin to live in another way. I don't say it to her, but I don't want to live another way: as much as the days and their movements may have become this torture, I want to keep living this way because this way I don't abandon her, because this way I live close to her. That isn't living, Gabriela told me one day—that was before, long before, she was talking about my being always shut in and writing things that never happened to people who never existed; to live is to do things, to achieve or to fail, but to do. Fine, not living then, surviving, transpiring, being; I transpire and I survive and if the price is remorse because it was her and not me, if the price is to imagine her own hell creating mine, I am ready to pay it and the higher it is, the closer to her I am going to feel. Not for that reason do I accept it with happiness, or even with resignation—I'm not a saint, I don't pretend to be, I don't want to be. I want to be what I am; if she is not here and there are no outings on the water or Shakespeare or necklace of sky blue beads, I want to be this unnamable embodied pain, I want to imagine what I do not remember, what Gabriela and people like Gabriela have been bringing to light. I want to see without ever having seen, I want to hear without ever having heard, I want to be where I have not been and will not be, I want to be in her house, Gabriela's house, where you can still smell her, in her bedroom when she slept, when she played, when she talked to friends, when she cried (why wouldn't she have cried?, at that age, everyone cries); when she studied, when they burst in while she tried to open the clasp of the sky blue bead necklace because she had just come in and she was going to change, take off her dress and her sandals, when they took her, they dragged her away while she screamed and one of them punched Gabriela in the stomach and she slid down against the wall to the floor unable to breathe, move her hands, question, ask for help, anything, because it was all useless. I want their boots to crush me the way they crushed her against the floor of the car in which they took her away and I want them to hit me in the head until my eardrums burst and in the gut until I vomit and bleed from the mouth. And none of this washes me clean of regrets or remorse or recriminations, nothing. Nor do I think seconding Gabriela would help me; more than that, I think what she does is abominable. Pain is political, yes, but it should be hidden, obscure. No one needs to know that when the walls recede and I begin once again this passage through the last days of her life, what I want to achieve is that she know that I love her. I am crazy, Gabriela, you're right, and I don't care: I care that they dragged her out of the car and carried her, anticipating the banquet—shouts and laughter—to that place you saw in blackened ruins. They threw her to the ground and they set her up on her feet, her little feet still wearing their sandals, and they shoved her into the heart of that abyss from which she would not come out, that knot from which the arms of the labyrinth divided, that room so octagonal it was almost round, in which the gestures, words, shouts, the howl, the guffaws, would remain forever, to be seen and smelled and heard, without ever being able to get out of there, stuck to the eight walls like diz-zying frescos of a hell that is renewed with every glance, room, sphere; a damp, cold, and windowless prison in which they stripped her naked and blindfolded her eyes and touching her and abusing her and enough, enough, I don't want to, I can't, it is impossible for me to follow her torment without feeling that the only solution is death. My death, not hers. Maybe in my last second of life I will be able to think, already without consciousness and without light, only a bunch of instinct, be able to construct another life and in that segment of eternity be certain she is alive and is at my side squeezing my hand cry-ing because I am leaving and yet here I am and she left and time is eternal, immobile, inclement and hard and I can only fill it with words. When I lack words, when words fail me, when they escape from the tips of my fingers, I remain here on the thresh-old of pain, in that damned heart of a room without windows, with eight sides and a door in each one, doors that lead to tor-ture and to death. And it is then I want to write the story of a woman who escapes all that; leave off stories of girls who want to be writers and men who don't know what they want; aban-don the great rivers and the deserts and the hidden tombs await-ing their prey and dead bodies under the floorboards of gaming rooms in far-away countries that have nothing to do with mine. It's something else, I want to write something else, perhaps to free myself from this thing, but I don't know if in writing about a woman who escapes what Chela-Chelita did not escape, I am going to be closer to her, or if by inventing the words that go with the story I am going to move further away from her in the worry about how to say things. What do I care about the how, that which matters to me above all else in the novels I construct (to use Gabriela's word), that which was paramount when life had not yet come to pieces and was still a path to be followed, a landscape to be contemplated? I want her not to have died and I don't know how to make her come back because I don't know how to do anything besides write novels that at one time I was proud of because they let me earn money and a kind of limited, domestic fame made up of interviews, notes in the papers, roundtables, flattering voices, signing copies at book fairs. What do I want, what? Other than to construct novels and accompany Chela-Chelita on her path toward death, what is it I want? Possibly nothing; nothing except that, over and over again. Possibly to construct, since I'm able to do that, a different world in which nothing is lost; in which all the imagined lives of the girl from England, of the little man amazed at events whose significance escapes him, of the raped and tortured girl with the necklace of sky blue beads around her neck, everything is preserved in an economy of souls that allows me, however it might be, to go back to her. Go back. Hold her once again in my arms, crying because she didn't pass the exam or happy because tomorrow she's going on vacation. Warm, in any case. Smelling of Charlie, bring me Charlie don't forget when you go through the duty free shop where it's cheaper. Will you remember? Free, different. No longer a chubby girl, all big eyes, whose hand I held so many times, taking her to kindergarten, now the woman I never got to know, the distant, obscure figure of the martyr torn apart in the arena, the sand stained with blood and fear. I know she was afraid. What do you know, Gabriela says. How could I not know? I spend my life inventing fear. I know, I know what she felt in the first torture session; I know, as she knew, where each passage led from its starting point in each one of the eight walls that delimited that space like a cold and abandoned tomb, a trap in which the beasts of this world were going to die roaring. But jaguars don't die just like that: they defend themselves, they go out by night to hunt, extend their claws, arch their backs and attack and one leaves this life trying to flee that attack. They reek of blood, of the lair, of thirst, of dismemberment achieved by blunt attack; of death and of death. They emerge triumphant where no one emerges, viscous remains in their jaws and a kind of roar, a purr of satisfaction in their throats. They have no fear: only the hereditary mandate of the great cats, gold and soot, that marks each elegant hide. And they attack. And kill. Maybe they die but they die nobly, among golden cloudscapes and lance points: they die fighting and leaving their own mark as well, so they are not forgotten. The naked girls, raped and tortured on the metal tables, don't die nobly. They have not been able to fight. They did not have claws and from those throats emerged only cries and whimpers. Remains. Remains in the jaws of the jaguars, in the story of those who killed them and left us not even their bodies, as if they had never existed, as if nothing had ever existed and everything had been, I won't say a novel, but perhaps a reflection of another world. Or perhaps novels are what one obtains with a gesture, one constructs novels as Gabriela says and at the same time one is constructing another world in which those things that don't happen do happen and are true and real. Why not? Why can't it be that way, why aren't words all-powerful as one so often says in interviews, because that is what others want to hear; why is it that dreamed-up worlds aren't the path our actions follow? I do something, I change my shoes or I eat fried potatoes or I write a novel and every grimace, gesture, smirk opens another world in which things are happening that would not have happened if I had not proofread chapter twenty-six. And every grimace, gesture, smirk, expression of anyone who lives in any one of those worlds and in this world, opens other worlds in each one of which all the gestures that are made are—well. That. A tree, that's it, a tree, a tree of worlds that my gestures can travel until they find one in which there is no absence and remain there, nested, curled up, closed up within myself so not a single strand might begin to once again unleash the story, the pitiless story of these years and I can be ready to go with her to Montevideo in the hydroplane for the symposium and neither she nor I ever, ever learn what a jaguar is. Let the jaguars die in the land of the great rivers and let me apply myself without pain to the all-powerful words that tell the lives of those who found themselves at the edge of the desert. The telephone, for instance: write how they made love that night for the first time, how almost without words, in a language that was not her language and that he was forgetting little by little, how he lifted her in his arms, so light, and carried her to the bedroom, his bedroom, not hers, which one had to climb three steps to enter, and how he left her on the bed and how she felt a second, just a second of terror until the image of Bridget, wounded, disappeared and the memory of all her plans was driven into her side like an animal made of grappling irons; and something like a heavy, fragrant cloak, soft and hot like the water in which life simmered for the first time, covered her so she could raise her arms and feel that this man who spoke to her in a low voice was what the yellow light and the bloodied face in the newspaper and the tea in the dining room and the voyage and the *curús* and the imagined deaths had predicted for her, reserved, destined in a secret place with eight sides and eight doors, that obscure place, heart of the house, for her, only for her. Tell how everything was, how suddenly the air she breathed changed and his hands searched urgently for the zipper, the buttons, whatever, and what she thought, felt, this is important, when her legs were no longer imprisoned in the tall boots, hard boots that protected her from the dangers that slithered beneath the rotten bark, from the sand and the wind and the brush against her thighs, and to know that while there is fever in the house and her womb blossoms and time stands still, at some moment the telephone is going to ring and she is going to call, let's go get a coca cola on this spectacular day or better yet an ice cream and you can have a coffee, just here at the corner or that place with the croissants, the one across from the botanical garden, come on, before I have to start studying, no, mom won't mind because she isn't here. Why, why can't I? Why is it impossible for me to die or to go crazy, to take that difficult and instantaneous step toward the darkness in which there is nothing any longer, not memories or imaginings or cities in the clouds or necklaces of sky blue beads or brutes that take her and throw her down on a hard cot and rape her, one by one—panting, laughing—they bleed her and afterward they say bring in another and carry this one to the machine but she is no longer herself, rather pure pain that shuts down the senses and even prevents her from hearing the music that covers the cries of the other, the one who follows, cries just like her own that she doesn't even know she cries, that she has cried. And from then on, the worst, what I cannot, what I don't want to imagine: did she call someone? did she ask for someone? did she ask for something? Death, maybe; she, too, may have asked for death, which was going to come to her slowly, too slowly, as if undecided, walking sideways, looking sideways—do I give you my gifts or not, the sweet illness, the tasty poison, the mild wound?—that which is like love in your arms and between your legs, that for which you have been begging, now, one more attack and I'll arrive, one more wail, that's it, like that, I'll be there soon, when you least expect, when you think I will not come, I will give you all the sea to drink, I will burn you with every fire, you will climb the mountain so the rock can roll again down to the plain, I will pass over your crushed body flattening it and leaving it wounded, the bones broken, bleeding holes where there were eyes, and I will arrive, I will arrive at last, ah, how grateful you are going to be when in that bit of a millisecond you realize I possess you at last, you are receiving me, lovingly surrounded with the little that remains to you of moist life made of saliva and blood and juices milk honey bleach Charlie cream river breath roar hydroplanes music coca cola ice cream and coffee on the coastal promenade and nothing more ever and to rest at last, to be able to turn over in bed and to sleep with one arm under the pillow the other hugging me don't leave on me no no I'm not going to leave you ever, I will always be in that black, heavy dream, as beneficent as a caress, murmuring like the purring of the great cats so that you can sleep that way, always, always, now without pain. That's how I want to die. I want to beg death to come to me the way she did, here I am, waiting for you like a lover; I dream that she arrives, a gentle lover with breasts white as little goats dark eyes like mines of gold and black sunshine, she seduces me, envelops me, possesses me, she whispers sweet words in my ear and she lifts me up to the deserted city in the clouds where I can sleep in a gigantic bed all to myself in which everything fits, Chela-Chelita and the dreams and chocolate and tame jaguars and blue rivers and all that I never wrote and that now I will not write because maybe it's not so difficult to die and in that instant, less than an instant, the words will no longer have power and meaning and I will sink into that namelessness which—is it possible?—once again I will be able to call happy, with the window open, a little bit of wind outside like a song or a sharp whistle, the telephone ringing uselessly and it will ring and ring and I'm looking for a mirror in front of which to see myself take the step that only those who promise themselves they'll be happy can take, a mirror in which to see myself until the last minute, the last second, not the end, not the last contortion, the last expression as I did not see her last spasm of pain, lids half closed over the now cold pupil, but to see myself and then afterward the true ending that will be like the beneficial nothingness that no longer even has a name, the unknown darkness of death, the image, my face, the disgust of the metallic taste in my mouth, the rough butt that uselessly grows warmer, like that, even more, pushing the barrel that also warms, grotesque, unwanted, infectious against the palate and between my lips while I squeeze, hard, effective, now without a soul, with my teeth so it will not move, will not disillusion me, and now yes, like that, let's go, my face in the mirror and her shadow behind me protesting because she has trouble opening the necklace clasp, to finally see myself and see her at last

RECOUNTING
from ZERO

Bruno Seguer

VANDERBILT UNIVERSITY PRESS
Nashville, Tennessee

How can I know what I feel?

JEANETTE WINTERSON

The Light, the Lights

SHE WOULD HAVE to do something, sometime, with that life, her life, and she did not know what that something was or what it was going to be or what it might be. True, she was still young to have figured out what she wanted. But her classmates, those blond girls with plump legs who hid their little laughs for just a second behind a cupped hand, they were also very young and many of them already knew, they had planned it and dreamed it and told their best friends in quiet voices. She was no one's best friend, but that doesn't mean they excluded her or stopped talking when she came in.

She was a different type of person, more distant, more unseeing, more in search of something she would not find—how could she not know that?—in the middle of life's path; she, although it didn't seem so, was herself isolated, she who was the untouched virgin because she wanted to be a virgin always and forever, because she couldn't stand the idea of being touched, of being brushed against even slightly: a hand, a flank, lips, anything as alive as the purity she carried as a banner. Many of those who already knew what they wanted to do mocked her, in a friendly way, amused by this zeal for purity. She didn't know what she was going to be, but she knew she was going to keep herself safe; she was going to remain alone, without anyone forcing her to do anything, without feeling obliged to make the least gesture to fulfill a body-to-body intimacy that she detested without ever having known it.

The house, her house, her parents' house where she lived, was like all the houses on that street and the people who lived in them were like the people in all the houses of that street of that city in which the cold, the soot, and the fog spoke in the ear of anyone, be they saints or sinners; they spoke of heroism and of ghosts, of the gas bill and the woman in the house across the street. The same, or almost the same, as what is spoken, told, heard in all the houses on all the streets in all the cities in the world, only colder, grayer.

Since the future was there, trembling and distant as if it had been the victim of a secret sacrifice, and since that was all and everything she knew, she thought she would go away and live in another house on another street in another city—but not another world, in this same world; she would go to other places, she would hear other voices, she would speak another language.

"I want to study languages," she said.

Anything to do with studying was fine with her family. What language did she want to study? German, French, Italian,

Spanish? One of them, several: she would choose two. And that is what she did and upon leaving school she went to the Institute of Foreign Languages and recited irregular verbs (impersonal, never redeemed) to speak of other actions that began and sometimes ended in other cities and she memorized prepositions that tied up other relationships (difficult, improbable) between other words that had other meanings.

Another tongue.

Another way of saying things, of requesting, commanding, asking, understanding, fighting, buying, selling, answering, arguing. With other people in other houses on other streets, any other streets so long as they were not these.

Good people, that father and mother of hers. Good people her sister and her two brothers as well. She wanted to leave, to not see them again, not hear them, not encounter every morning's honeyed sweetness. That zeal to go to another part of the world where she would not have to run into her people morning, noon, and night and have to say hello, offer explanations, smile and feel she was wasting time in a swamp of fussiness, that was a good place to begin to finish finding out what she was going to do, be, how, when. But it wasn't much and meanwhile she kept living, going to school, learning languages, two of them for the moment.

She didn't like them, her family. It wasn't that she didn't love them; she did love them a little and even enough to suppose that if one of them died she would feel great sorrow. But no one was going to die: all the days seemed the same, although of course there were Christmases, sicknesses, surprises, vacations. The days varied at Christmas, for example, when there were gift packages wrapped in shiny paper, or when surprise intervened because a wedding invitation arrived, or when someone was sick and it was necessary to be silent and await the doctor's visit (had they put clean towels in the bathroom?). Or during vacations when the sea moved as if it were calling her. The voice of the sea made her almost happy. Christmas gifts, too, and surprises. Sickness, no, but sicknesses passed and when they had passed she could run down the stairs again clattering the soles of her shoes against the wooden steps. She didn't like them because she tried to make them understand something and they didn't understand: they approved with a smile without even knowing what the hidden, underground map of things was like. She searched not only behind words but beneath expressions and on the other side of dreams and they said only, *how nice, dear*. And she felt they were cheating her.

The days, the ones that weren't sick days or Christmas or vacation, all seemed the same. But the most painful hour was dusk and especially in winter when the light was unredeemable. The house grew dark, slowly, that was the saddest part: slowly. The darkness from outside came as if on four short, padded feet—or no, it would be better to say slithered, mild and slow; it climbed the entrance stairs, passed under the door, spread itself like a blanket on the floor, covered the furniture, climbed up the walls and then someone, usually her mother, would say:

"Turn on the lights."

She preferred not to be home at that hour, but some days, it was unavoidable. When the house squandered its colors and became silent, as silent as someone who has lost all interest in the life they are living, then she would have liked to be somewhere else. Sometimes she was in the school library, or at a friend's house, or in the park, or doing the weekly shopping that she and her sister did by turns, or simply on the run from the mere thought of that semi-dark part of the day when the walls become dull and there arises a more than uncertain correspondence between the corrupted light and the silences.

She didn't want to be the one to turn on the lights because that was even sadder than seeing the darkness arrive. Someone turned the porcelain button on the wall beside the door and the lights came down, they didn't rise like the darkness, they came down and tinted everything with that yellow powder that came from the last movement of the sun and when her father arrived he looked suspiciously at that ash that floated seamless and almost invisible above the shelves and the telephone and the picture frames and he said:

"See if you can't turn off a few lights, we don't need so many."

At that hour, if she was at home, she tried to shut herself in her room and do the homework for Spanish or German or whatever language she was studying.

And it was because of that, because of that combination of sadness, darkness, yellow fog in front of her eyes and on top of things, it was because of that she learned something about herself. Little by little, too, slithering, too, like the darkness, and because she had read Chesterton and Muriel Spark in school and Cervantes and Pérez Galdós and the formidable Pardo Bazán and Schiller and Heine and Heinrich Böll at the Institute, she told herself one day she would write books like those; she told herself that now she knew what she wanted to do, to be in her life.

Still, she never had a thought or a gesture of gratitude toward the light, the lights; toward the darkness and sadness. Just as well, because the corollary of all that discovery was her inevitable departure. She would leave.

I Want to Live with Myself

MEANWHILE, FROM THE other side of the world—not so much the other side, more toward the south, toward the world's equatorial belt—the owner of La Preciada gave orders to finish covering the canoes and tying up the animals, *let's go! let's go!* because the storm was threatening. The air smelled of water, and it wasn't the water of the river, it was water from the sky, the water of the cities in the clouds, the omnipotent water of the beginning of everything. It was coming, it was coming, and he bellowed more than the wind and dust got into his eyes and jaws, *quickly, it's on its way, let's go!*

The wind from the west raised cloudbursts of sand that beat at the trunks of the enormous trees (spongy, dark) and knocked to the ground the spiny shrubs, the plants full of tempting, velvety, inedible fruit; the wind, a wind almost permanently garnet-hued, dark, the voice of an opened womb and the strength of animals that rise up in spite of the weather, in spite of the huddled man, the hidden sun, the wind that beats against the house.

In spite of the strength of the wind and the first enormous drops that foretell the invincible deluge to come, irreparable in spite of the foresight and the determination with which he tries to overcome dejection, everything has been covered with the waterproof canvas, the piled-up bales, the canoes tied to the dock, the animals under the roof of braided straw tied to wooden beams. The men run to find shelter and he, slowly, as if studying what carries him along, as if the rain were not tormenting him or the wind groping his flesh and his hair, he moves, almost calmly, toward the house.

The house. It is impossible not to speak of that house beside the monstrous river of which one cannot see the other shore.

"That which you see, that is not the other shore. Those are the islands and further on the streams that lead to the delta, kilometers and kilometers further downstream. Afterward, with luck, one can go out into the green sea and when I say sea I'm not saying water, not yet; I'm saying that even to reach it one has to cross all that foliage, those fronds that sink their roots in the water of the river and try to prevent one from reaching the destination. That, that which you see."

The water gets choppy with the storm but it doesn't speak the way the sea speaks. This is the river, the water muddy and sweet, there are whirlpools and unsuspected channels; at the bottom hide snub-nosed fish with hooked tails and there are plants with gray leaves that serve as food for the alevins when they emerge from the transparent eggs. The river murmurs at night and by day if someone falls quiet in the middle of a sentence and some-times when it grows choppy it doesn't speak, it hollers in time with the squall.

The house is made of wood, wide battens of reddish, rough-hewn wood, protected by the putty knife that goes back and forth, over and over, that soaks the knots with the gum released when trees die and that begins to give it shape, smoothing, squeezing against the roughness that resists it. It's strong, as it has to be to endure the sun and the winds and now and again the water of the storms that come from the west.

And it is huge, surrounded by a wide gallery supported by piles, also wooden, that support a sloped roof. One enters at the front through a double door secured at night with two bars held at the jambs by padlocks. In the rear part of the house, giving onto the corridor that connects the offices with the living room, there is another door that opens onto the gallery and is seldom used. It takes work to open it and when it does open the hinges squeak as if with fatigue or anger. The openings have bars and wire screens against mosquitos, flying insects, and bats.

The rooms look out through tall, narrow windows, also pro-tected, that open onto the gallery. There is only one that does not have windows and it is exactly in the center of the house. It is so octagonal, it is almost round. Dark, empty, not large, it serves as passage or antechamber to the bedrooms. Two, each one with its bath. If the house as a whole has a certain rustic, fortress-like air, the baths are of recent construction, with white fixtures and impermeable floors; with hot and cold water in the pipes that serve the faucets, with showers, bathtubs, folding screens, and tiles on the walls.

Not so the kitchen, which is spacious, much more so than either of the baths, primitive, rustic. In the center of the large, rectangular space is a wooden table with benches at the sides. Pots and pans and copper kettles hang from racks on the walls. There is a utensil rack with hooks for strainers, skimmers, spatulas, and ladles. There is an enormous hearth in one of the walls and woodstoves and an oven for bread and meat.

The house has a dining room, a living room, two bedrooms, two offices, two other rooms that serve for guests or as workrooms. More the second than the first, because rarely, if ever, are guests received. The two bedrooms are spacious, with high ceilings and plank floors. One of them is at the level of the nearly round anteroom. One must climb three steps to reach the other. The bedroom windows are also protected with grilles and wire mesh. They have no curtains. At dawn the low sun reflects an orange light over the walls of those two rooms. As morning advances, the light becomes brighter, almost white, and it moves across the floor until the gallery roof blocks the sun and the two rooms remain cool and shadowy until night when everything is definitively dark.

Because there is no electric light in the house. There was once, when La Preciada had a different owner and was no more than a precarious jetty, the unfinished house, and two huts for the workers; there was a generator that now rusts beside the water tower and was never repaired or replaced. Water, there, is more important than light. For that reason there is a tank that can hold fifty-thousand liters, fed by the river and by the rains, and a wood-fired boiler that heats the water for the kitchen and the baths. The water climbs up to the tank by means of a pump operated by hands and arms. The men call the alert and five or six come and they establish rotations. One by one they operate the pump and long ago a kind of competition developed among them to see who can endure longer, pumping water upward. To light the house, there are kerosene or oil lamps, and candles in brass or pewter candlesticks. The kerosene and the oil come in metal cans brought by the canoes that come down from the plains to La Preciada in search of bales or in some cases bundles, depending on the cargo.

He thinks about fatigue. Not the fatigue he feels, fatigue in general. Outside, the storm seems to be abating. He doesn't think about the fatigue he feels, though he is certainly tired. And it is likely the storm is as well, although she will leave the field and he will not. He has been through many storms: in one of them he was at the point of death, trapped between a cart flipped over by the wind on the bank of the river and the indifferent water that seeped into his clothes and his boots and was sinking him, heavy and unable to move his arms or his legs, hopeless, into the mud. In another storm, a fast, treacherous one that left no time for anything, he lost the whole cargo he had ready, baled and bundled, with the seals and the destination labels on, waiting beside the dock for the boat that announced itself, still far off, with the hoarse voice of the whistle. If from that near death it had taken him some hours to recover and forget the sensation of water seeping inexorably between his clothes and his body, the ever more oppressive weight awakened by his own movements as he tried to save himself, it took him three months to recover from—not forget—the loss of the cargo; or perhaps he did forget, but not entirely.

The others are all the same or at least become confused in memory: the sky grows crimson, most times streaked with dark blue locks that melt into a reddish tone, the horizon rises up, the leaves don't move and the insects don't buzz and the birds don't sing and the dogs don't bark and old Tuca dries her hands on her apron and crosses herself. One of the plainsmen who always hangs around the kitchen, his name is Reusileo, or something like that, asks for salt and pours it in a ring around two knives crossed in the dirt. The storms, nonetheless, come despite the knives and the fear and the salt, and they pass through and move on and things remain as before, only a little messier, and it feels as if everything must begin again from the beginning.

It is only an impression, but it wears down the spirit— although he asks himself, in that moment of reflection on fatigue, if it might not be that everything, everywhere, the very work of time, gives that sensation of eternal beginning. Until one has nothing left, he thinks, until one resigns oneself, which is the worst that can happen to anyone.

It moved on, the storm finally passed and the water of the river returned to stillness, only apparent but stillness, and the men began to come out of the shacks and took the protection off the canoes so as to continue wrapping up the bales.

Heliotropes

SHE BOASTS TO herself, she pretends, she persuades: she is going to be a writer, she is going to write books, seated at an unpolished wooden table in a comfortable armchair with a crimson velvet seat. There will be a very tall, dark bookcase filled with books in front of her, there will be antique prints on the walls. A single lamp on her desk, source of a very white light that will never reach as far as the faded walls, and the rest in shadows.

How is it possible that she knows what she wants if she has barely touched on a hazy desire? She doesn't know it all, because what she does not yet know for certain—how could she?—is when or how, how to get there.

But she knows, she sees it as if it were before her eyes, she knows that in the books she is going to write she will speak of tormented souls, of arduous journeys to strange lands, of mis-understandings, unexpected visits, of the life that reawakens, of unspeakable secrets, of desolation and sadness, of men and women who expect something magnificent from their own destinies, of catastrophes, injustices. Of death that erases everything.

She knows vaguely what she will call those things that slide by on the page, she knows a lot; not everything, but a lot. She knows what is waiting for her, she knows that days and months will pass before she can sit down at that unpolished wooden table. Years, too—no, not years, she doesn't want to think about that. She tells herself she doesn't care, it is the price she has to pay and it's a reasonable price, a price in time, a hemisphere, a crystal egg marked with the hours when the sun comes through the gap, silent by day, sorrowful, absent when it is night. It is a comfort to be able to think about the crystal fragility of the hours and in the meantime flee from the house when the evening darkness arrives.

Outside, in the world, there is no way to measure the sun, no way to watch it move through half-closed eyelids. She sees it as if it were the collector, on the rebound, of shadow and suspicion, sees it without knowing anything of the color it takes on. The sky with its clouds, the cut crystal egg—silently cut in the ghetto by some solitary lens maker—all of this belongs to her more than any object, more than her decisions and her refusals.

More than her steps. What will her steps be like when she leaves? What crack will echo with the soles of shoes that are no longer those that descended the staircase after sickness? And when she writes about death, will it be some death she has already wit-nessed? She has not seen death. She has seen, yes, the meetings, and she has seen the men and the women who believe this is the day on which they will do something magnificent with their lives. But what about her? Will she write about herself?

She can say nothing about herself, but she wonders if the words she is going to trace, someday, the day on which something magnificent is going to happen, if the words she is going to trace won't be she herself; if the letters won't reproduce her face, if her voice won't echo in the spaces. And if in the final period there will not be a voice that answers hers.

Strange devices, imagined by strange, wise men shut up in towers or in dungeons, devices that will be the crystal egg that measures the sun, or the words that will appear at the movement of her wrist, when her fingers seize up around the pen, when the ink smells of the water in which the iron is to be tempered, that miracle of the loaves and the fishes that produces steel.

She knows, in the convexity of the crystal, other worlds can be seen.

Cervidae

VERY EARLY IN the morning, the sun wakes him, shining between knots of wire and dreams. The sun that comes from the other side of the storms, from the east that is cloudless and nearly always right between reddish and yellow; it falls on his face and settles on his chest until he opens his eyes. He thinks of coffee, he invariably thinks of coffee when he wakes up, but water has first claim and, naked and thirsty but never barefoot, he goes to the bath and lets the water run.

The first stream is brown, like the river water, not muddy but brown with whatever the pipes drag along after a dry day. He knows he has to let the water run and jump and spatter until it settles down and becomes clear. He feels, but this time without knowing it completely the way he knows about the water, a certain strangeness before the petty things that could become threatening or could foretell big changes. Life, he says to himself, doesn't change, and he looks at the water. Coffee, the smell of coffee. After the sun and the water will come the coffee and after that Osmán will be waiting for him in the big office with all the papers on the table, invoices, remittances, receipts, bills, and budgets. They need to buy canvas. Last night there was a roundup and the men returned this morning exhausted: they will have to hire temporary workers.

"Take the raft," he tells him, "go to the Pearl Co. office and see if they have people available. Don't let them fill up the return space."

"That," says Osmán, "will take all morning."

"There's no other choice. Or is there?"

"No."

"Go, then, and try to have them give you people experienced with shipments. If we have them, we'll meet Saturday's deadline."

Osmán says goodbye and goes out. The morning opens for him face to face like a golden door.

Sometimes he misses the sound of a piano. There is no piano in the house, no instrument for making music, but he misses music because he was born and grew up in a house where a flute or a violin or a piano was always playing. In Dresden, when he was a boy, he was sure music was solid, hard as a dart, able to pierce the walls of houses and fly out to the street just when he was passing. He never played an instrument, not he, but he was accustomed to the presence of music in his house, in others' houses, in public squares. So, should he bring a piano? What a crazy idea.

Osmán will return at midday or, if they delay him at Pearl's, in the afternoon. It's an inconvenience: it will be necessary to work hard, much harder than on normal days, and every time that happens, he already knows, people get tired and complain and even abandon the task.

Yes, every time. Every time there is a roundup there are problems the next day. Before, years before, it happened now and again. At six month intervals, more or less. But now it was a matter of every fifteen or twenty days at the most—hardly a month. Osmán had explained that back then, in the times of the gringo Culberstone, the thing was exclusive. Osmán had worked for Culberstone, as a boy and as a youth—that Osmán had ever been a little boy seemed beyond incredible—when the place was an inhospitable hole overflowing with mud and they put up a sorry campaign tent on the highest ground, opposite the water, back when you had to go into the river to load the canoes that would carry bales and bundles to the boats because there wasn't even a worm-eaten plank to use as a pier.

In contrast now all the tribes were included in the call and the men left the shacks at dusk like ants going hunting far from the anthill and they went in search of what each tribe had to offer. He that found a place and a wife never came back, but those who returned standoffish and beaten, they were the ones who had been judged and rejected because they had committed an offence, a misdemeanor, or because they had been caught in disobedience. And there were others that returned, the majority: the defeated, those who had achieved nothing, who had not been looked upon favorably because they were not of the tribe, not of a suitable family; they returned exhausted and indifferent and it took them three or four days to recover.

A piano. Music that would pierce the walls when he passed. He used to think, when the aroma of coffee flooded the house and reached his bedroom, he used to think the sun was a kind of music.

He was faintly aware that he himself was hardened, burnt out, dry but—although he did not know it—on the verge of discovering that the fragile thicket he had been building over many years had worn down, it seemed now to be made of frosted glass and it was ready to break; for that reason he could not have thought of personifying, that is to say musicalizing, the sun. There has to be something else, not exactly that. Something that makes the sun put within his reach—treacherously, wavering, Faustian and thieving—the memory of music, of his steps in the snow (the snow! snow, that white, that thing like mint and crystal), of the hollow walls and the prospect of his own destiny.

At times it seemed to him it was the sun more than the wind that tore sounds from the sand, from the trees and the water of the river. With the few men who had not been part of the roundup he made a recount and inspection of the bundles. Canvas? What had Osmán said about canvas? He concluded that they would get to Saturday and when the large boat came down, they would—with effort, granted—but they would be able to make the delivery with all the bales in good condition.

If Osmán brought temporary laborers, untrained as they might be, and if they could rouse any of those who had returned from the roundup, it was even possible La Preciada could load its own vessel. It was unlikely. Unlikely because they had tried other times without success to rouse those who had returned from a roundup, and because those who had not returned by now would not be back. Who wants to return if they have a wife, princess or dancer or water carrier or weaver or whatever she might be? A wife with an untroubled brow, that is, without the fangs of brown desert rats hanging from the woven headband, who smiled and who played the piano, for him.

He heard the midday bell: it echoed even on the river.

Perpetual Motion

AT FIVE SHE left the office with a coworker who suggested they have a drink before going home.

"It's Friday," she said.

All the same, on a Friday and with the last of the sun (sticky, timid, almost begging) she did not want to go anywhere. She said they were expecting her at home, something about a visit, something like that, and said goodbye.

Three blocks to the subway entrance, and for those three blocks she thought only about figures, she placed them one after the other, some below others, she subtracted, she added, she divided, she counted them up and made them sing to find out for sure whether they weren't hiding another voice, and she realized how mistaken she had been. Her time was slipping away and in her room, in the desk drawer, she had only six or seven pages she couldn't bring herself to throw in the wastebasket and a few bills in an envelope under her lingerie. She couldn't go like that, with nothing, she couldn't go yet. Go where? Go. Go somewhere, far, that's it, far away, where a place awaited her in which she could write her books about tormented lives, miserable characters, frustrations, distant lands she has never seen, the impossibility of love, death that erases everything.

A different job, she had to look for a different job that paid more so she could save. When she set foot on the first step going down, she was no longer the person she had been, she was a determined witness to her own self, who knew, who had just discovered—no longer in the blurry depths of her soul but right here in front of her eyes—that it was impossible, the effort was impossible. Unless, she told herself. She saw far off in the tunnel the train's light. Unless, unless she were able to find a job in which writing were obligatory. Librarian? Not a secretary, nor a teacher. She boarded the train. Writer. But there are no jobs as a writer.

She would write that, someday she would write about the impossibility of writing. A woman in an unnamed country seated at an unpolished wooden table trying to give form, in words, to that, to the frustration, the impossibility of loving, the rancor, the perilous rancor.

She bought a newspaper at the subway exit. There was only one left at the newsstand and it wasn't exactly among the most serious. Scandals, bloody axe-murderers, shameless divorces, civil servants suspected of giving a Mercedes to a stripper, turmoil in aristocratic families, wandering inheritances, all of that and more. What did she care? There, on the sunless sidewalk under the eaves, by the light of a shop window, she looked for the classified page. Employment—Openings. No, she didn't want to be a secretary, nor a cashier, a bookkeeping assistant, a maintenance worker, none of that which in the end was worse than what she already had. Domestic Service—Openings, just in case some old lady lost in a cloud of oblivion needed someone to read Trollope to her. No. Not that either. She folded the paper and carried it under her arm because she didn't find a wastebasket to throw it in. Two blocks to the north, half a block to the right, cross the street and she was at her house and the lights were already on and her father had arrived and had declared it necessary to save on the light bill.

"A teacher doesn't earn enough for luxuries."

She climbed up to her room, newspaper still under her arm. She threw it in the wastepaper basket beside her desk, folded in quarters, with a bloodied face clearly visible and a screaming headline of which all she could see was the word butcher.

Bad omen: face covered in blood, dirty paper among her papers, which she always wanted neat, even the throwaways: folded once and then again so as to show that? She took off her coat, put away her purse, she sat down, waiting for something to happen in the house, something that would have nothing to do with her because she was no longer there; she was but she was not. She would leave. Waiting for a call or an accident, whatever it might be, anything, and meanwhile the word butcher was there as if for no other reason but that she should look at it.

She took the newspaper out of the basket and opened it so as to fold it a different way and not have to see the word or the blood or the face. Openings—Various. Let's see what Various means.

Invisible, Unapproachable

SOME DAY SHE would write an epistolary novel, a novel in which only the woman's letters could be read and it would never be known to what she was referring, what questions she was answering, why she said what she said. A novel just from that edge of life, in which it would be the mystery and not the assertion that jumped out at the reader. The woman writing those letters in the novel she writes, she alone would know, only she, whether anyone spoke to her from the other side. There might be, perhaps, nothing. There might be, perhaps, within that which was not said, a desert of dust and sand where nothing could survive. Perhaps an interlocutor. Perhaps not. Perhaps bodies that dried out little by little, not for lack of water but for lack of memories, of intentions, of a need to return to what they had been. Perhaps that is called resignation. Perhaps it has no name but yet a power over the flesh, beyond the ability to speak and to gesture and even the capacity to say no and to go back—go back where?—as if that mattered. He knows that the beneficent heavens, the blue and white crockery, the darts of music are powerless when it comes to doing all the everyday things in different ways each day. She, on the other hand, that's what she wants. She wants to flee the yellow light, the watery sounds of waking; she wants, above all, to know the exact details of what will be, although she knows, she knows from thinking about it, that it is possible nothing might be as she repeats it, each exhalation a refrain. Her life, the life in the desert, the life of those people who would always be strange to her, is linked to the painful breath of work, to effort, to the conviction that everything will remain in the shadows, that when, as Pastor Häppfen said, the cold came to the world, nothing would mean anything. Only (it isn't certain but it's probable), what he aspired to would be to await that cold, the cold of the lighthouse at the end of the world that would burn until the air condensed around it. She had never in her life seen a lighthouse and she imagined it would be a tall tower from which she could see her life and decide, alone and strong, without regret, where and how, in what fashion to take up the pen, how to twist it over the paper so that the strokes would not all be the same but rather the opposite, thick, those that go up and down; delicate, barely visible, those that connect the letters that connect the words. How, otherwise, to bring to light a different world that shakes her, that through her arm, hand, fingers, pen, the fragrant black ink, causes someone to look up and ask themselves what this ground on which they live is really like? How, otherwise, to find out something of the other, the one who crosses the path, who speaks, the one who betrays, the one who dies? The wind from the west, which brings the rains, sometimes brings as well the scent of cities, the metallic scent of carcasses rotting in corners while men dressed in gray and women tousled by the breeze believe that in all things an unchanging order can be achieved. The howl of the desert dogs, hearing that alone would be enough for them to know—at least try to know—whether what they carry in their hands and in their pockets is what they have always desired. The desert squeezes throats and puts out fires. The bitter taste of coffee sticks to the palate for hours; steps on the sand leave ephemeral tracks that are wiped away with the breeze along with fallen branches and the harsh time that is passing, the infertile time, the time that gives no quarter. She knows it; she can linger in what she has never lived, in what she is willing to cross, in that which can be written and not sung, in the ignorance of the fabulous and the real, in the smooth vertical border of the sheets of poster board, in what she will never now be able to repair, in the thicket of the days and of the hours, in the moment, that moment that is going to arrive; she knows, she knows: it is going to arrive.

The Mask of Theory

ONE CAN NEVER be certain of what those men, those women, think. So different, so absent, so seemingly indifferent to everything and then suddenly they do what one never would have expected them to do. Dance, for example. Or they steal or they go away or go crazy and howl or they work like beasts of burden without rest and show themselves proud of what they have done or they even become irresistibly sensible and pose questions of economics or of religion.

At times—often, to tell the truth—he has tried to change places: let's see, if I were one of them and not who I am, how would *that* I see me? How would I see the world? What would I feel at nightfall? What images would I see before I fell asleep?

Not Dresden, surely, not festivals or crystal snow and lemon and mint on palate and fingers. He would feel, yes, it is more than probable, he would feel the dry wind of the desert as a gift and it would not occur to him that the wind off the dunes and the water of the river, brothers, were anything else, distinct one from another, were anything else, it would not occur to him that they were anything other than signs, traces of something he would be unaware of and that would come loose from the white paint on the faces of their women or the leathery leaves of the black tree against the setting sun. Perhaps he wouldn't care, but he thinks he would. If he were one of them it would matter to him or, who knows, would mean something, a guide, a formulation to which the hours or the food or clothing or whatever might be adapted. The weapons to carry on the hunt, for example. A rule, a model. Perhaps for the Abu'nakues nature would speak a different language than it spoke to the Chetvas and in that case the lives of those men would not be so simple, so elemental as he had wanted to believe. Work, sleep, eat, lie with women, that was what he would always believe was all they wished for, because that way he spared himself the risk of having to distinguish them one from another, to look at them attentively, take care when he spoke. What he would always believe was what opened the chasm between them. It is not Dresden, it is not the longing for a piano, it is not what he recognizes with the skin of his fingertips. It is that, it is the inability to stop being who he is so as to be another self who might see him just as he is.

He knows now (so many years have passed), he knows now, and this suits him, that the best he can do is leave them in peace. In that, he has to admit Osmán has been a great help. He remembers when he became impatient and attempted the impossible. The impossible would have become possible, desirable, in Dresden, but not here, in this place which is not even a hamlet, a ring of sun and fog and water around a house, a tower, three shacks.

But yet, ah, yet. He would have to drink another cup of coffee, wet the back of his neck with cold, cold water, stop himself thinking of impossibilities; but although there was a time, that one, the first, when he felt the flow of his own blood in his arms and above all here, below the sternum and here, in the lower abdomen; when each day he felt he would do something special, extraordinary, which would oblige those moments that mark a destiny—he didn't dare say a life—to contort, it is certain too that he himself had worn away that slope, that hillside, from so much going up and down without finally ever making of it what he needed to (he is not very sure what that is) so as not to erase it completely. He was like a wild animal, not domesticated, all tooth and growl, that comes and goes every day and night from the den to the stream stepping in the same tracks left the night before on the soft ground. The sand, he knows, does not preserve tracks. The wind glides over the sand, and over the sand go the men when he needs them most. He would have to, that's what he wants, drink another cup of coffee. And have prey to hunt. Sabre-toothed tigers, boa constrictors. But no, instead of the great lizards, instead of horrible cats, snub-nosed fish and those amber yellow bugs that run by night on swift feet with their transparent young on their backs, claws raised, liquid in their venom sacs and in their stingers, blind but aware of the slightest rumor, the minimal rustle that will justify coming out from under the rotten bark. Who wants to dirty their boot soles stomping bugs, or skewer themselves on the river's spines, or slip on the sand or sink into the mud, who can dream of that or try to conquer it?

In this wild, excessive land, it is best to be a scorpion or a tiger, a jaguar; best not to know and not to try to know. Know what?

Nothing. Know what has to be done with the cargo, what to pay, what to charge, just that, whatever's brewing but nothing more. Know how to speak to the men, distinguish members of one tribe from those of another, to learn, at most, a few words in the language of the forest dwellers and a few of those of the plains and a few of those of the nomads, who are the wildest, those who come least to La Preciada. He needs people who will scoop everything up and carry it off; he remembered that, thinking of the nomads, because the nomads are the strongest, big strong grim fellows who seem tireless, able to lift a whole cargo just opening and closing their arms. The nomads are the ones who suit him best for that work. But he has few and the few he has are already impatient and he knows why. He also needs balers; it isn't that he doesn't have them but those he has are plainsmen and it's well known the plainsmen are difficult people, people who do unexpected things like smile or keep quiet when one asks them to move. It's hard to communicate with them. He has offered to build them another shack, with interior walls so they can bring their women with them, but no. They smile, if those are smiles, and say nothing: they prefer to come and go, one week yes, the other no, and return and bale and continue without saying anything. He has not even been able to learn as many words from them as from the others. As with the nomads, it is almost all gestures, almost all noises and shouts, never words.

That land, oh, that hardly welcoming land that at one time he even thought he loved. Back then, everything was still to be done and his project was to bring what he called civilization and to live, days of courage and nights of black skies, surrounded by objects and sounds that once had been familiar; and instead, that land was swallowing him little by little.

He would drink, why not, another cup of coffee. He goes to the river, looks at the water, paddles (wishing he were elsewhere) toward the springs where he knows, although he never got so far north, knows there is a port, a true port from which to embark. One moment. And the impossible? He could not, he knows, could not, no matter how much he might look at that seed of a project inside and out, that which was nothing yet, he could not go back.

It is hotter in the kitchen than it is outside, a viscous heat that emerges in the form of smoke, steam, from the pots on the fire. He asks for coffee at the moment the whistle of the mission boat sounds outside. He indicates to Tuca that she should go out and call the first man she finds in the gallery and he tells him in a rush to ask the boatman to bring what he has for La Preciada, to help him, if he's bringing a lot and another person is needed, and to invite him to the kitchen to have coffee.

In the gallery there are two chests, a package, two sacks, and the man from the boat sits down at the kitchen table, leaves the lightest load on the floor, offers a greeting and stretches out his hand toward the jug of coffee passed by Tuca who, smiling, fat, dressed like a man, agile fingers, undoes the packets and spills the newspapers across the table.

Stature

THE BLOODIED FACE has remained there, installed maybe not forever but for interminable days that can't bring themselves to erase it except with whatever the long voyage to the south might bring. She took the newspaper out of the wastebasket and unfolded it so as to fold it again without the face, something she did not do because, on the last page, unfolded, she saw the featured notices. Maybe someone was looking for a writer, room and board, six hours a day at the unpolished wooden table, salary, a day off every week. No one is asking for writers. They ask for call-girls, waitresses, singers, escorts, accompanists, tour guides, seamstresses, dancers. Someone is asking for a wife. There are two looking for wives: one is seventy-three years old, retired from business, attractive, owner of a station wagon and a house in the suburbs, seeks a wife no older than forty, send details, measurements, and a recent photograph. The other. Come on, the other is, let's see, how old, ah, and asks for—what is he asking for? what does he need? The walls dissolve, dust and fog before her eyes and what has been behind—the gray street, the houses the same as all the other houses—all of that has disappeared and in its place the sand sparkles, the wind blows, there is a beautiful white house with polished floors and marble and barefoot servants with loose black hair and colored bead necklaces on their breasts and one can smell the wind bringing the night from the south.

What has most affected her is the part about "the land of the great rivers."

But if one marries, she has to. No, she won't be able to. In the land of the great rivers a man walks around and she watches him, under the stars of a continent she never expected to see, and that man thinks, he imagines that someone imagines him, he believes that in some part of this world, not another one but this one, there is a woman who bought a newspaper and at this moment takes a fountain pen and a blank sheet of paper out of her desk drawer and moistens the pen in the inkwell and without being very sure of what she does, as if playing a game, telling herself all this is not important and will go no further, writes a reply.

She read what she had written carefully, paragraph by paragraph. She knew she could never, in the event she received an answer, continue with this. Up to here, and that will be all. She knew she could not be married, not she, because she has wanted to be alone always.

A married woman, she, absent from her own world, she, attuned to another body, what is it that a married woman does? What hands, what mouth? How to demur? She did not want, not in any way, to imagine that man that imagines her, imagine him in three dimensions turning toward her and stretching his hands out, always looking at her, nowhere else, at her. To think of him in the land of the great rivers, in that house where, seated at an unpolished wooden table, she could write about the desolation and the unspeakable secrets and of how even in the most complete happiness there is a trace of desperation that defeats anyone who touches it. She wanted to write that and she thought for a moment about the first words, the first line of the first page of a book in which she would say something about death. She would begin with death so as to then go backward, like that, without knowing very well what she was doing, as if it were a game.

She wouldn't be able to go toward death with the memory of a man lying at her side, the darkness, a hand that gets tangled up at her shoulder and, catching the strap, slides it down her arm. Do men speak when they take possession of a woman? Do they say anything? What do they say? What syllables, what verses, what murmurings? Does their tongue loll like when they get drunk? Do they know what they're saying? Or is everything the same, a hanging bridge from one waist to the other, stock of a forest in which they have battled uselessly since before she, the city, the world opened their eyes, smelled the wind? And the brush, the brush of fingers tearing off skin as they pass. Because they must burn, those fingers, those hands must burn the skin over which they pass and she perhaps might escape, might trickle away like water under the other body and she would get to her feet, finally alone once more. She didn't want poems or painstaking care, nor those eyes that are going to look at her, smiling, nor the complicit night. She didn't want anything, she only thought about the words with which she was going to announce the death and about the startled eyes of readers she would never see.

She stood beside the desk and looked down at the finished letter, still without a signature. For a second, less than a second, the bloodied face passed by her like a tiny wind and it made her think about revising the letter, about saying yes of course I am willing but you should never touch me, ever, which is nonsense because a man who lives in the land of the great rivers, alone, wants a wife precisely so he can touch her, a big man's body, and to seek solace and calm and she could not, could never, in spite of the bloodied face, she could never stand that.

She can remember what she never lived. She asks herself if that isn't the material thanks to which we exist. She is undecided because, although thinking about an embrace repels her, she remembers what she hasn't experienced and the phrases she has put in the letter. She doesn't say she doesn't want him to touch her. Only the absolutely necessary, and even with a little humor. "In any event," she says, "writing a letter to choose a wife is a little like running a race without knowing where the finish line is." She knows nothing about the men who go running out by the light of the moon in search of the wives the tribes have to offer. There are many women in the tribes, in all of them, and there are not many men because men run greater risks and when wombs are required, well—but she doesn't know all that, although when she finds out, she is going to do something that no one, she least of all, would have expected.

What she does at that moment, what she did expect and knew she was going to do, is to tear up the unsigned letter, make a ball of the scraps and throw it in the basket—not that it stops the bloodied face from looking at her, now no longer from the basket but in her memory instead.

Real, Unreal, and Indescribable

OSMÁN WAS THE first to see her.

"It has to be that one," Osmán thought, but he didn't say anything nor did he look at him.

"Is it that one?" the man asked.

"Perhaps," said Osmán.

No one had yet gotten out of the boat. The men had scarcely begun to struggle with the landing stage, amidst shouts and a whirlwind of arms and confusion about where each one belonged.

"It must be. There's no other white girl on the boat."

"She's very, very young."

He heard that, somewhere between surprised and dismayed. It was unusual that Osmán should make such a comment: he never (almost never) risked an adjective.

He hurried, went toward her. She who is looking at him.

She is married to this man. She has not yet seen death but death has passed by, brushing her, circling her and for that reason, she says to herself, only for that reason is she there. The sun has taken her by surprise: she never thought the sun could be so powerful, that the sun could strike, shake the world and make it wobble, raise itself up as owner of the earth; she, who comes from the fog and the cold and the gray sky, she, who doesn't know whether to wave, offer her hand, say something to him. She is tired of him and of everything because death passed by just barely touching her. She knows, she has been thinking about it during the journey, that if it were not for that she would not be under such a cruel sun. She would still be on the green and gray island believing that what she does is no more than a game, playing that she writes the letter and doesn't expect an answer, and that if the answer arrives, she will do nothing more, ever. Nothing.

She doesn't even remember having thought that the hand of death is less scorching than the hand of a man lying beside her. She didn't have to decide that yes, she would go, that was the moment.

She left as soon as Bridget started to get better, to speak, to say words, to cry sometimes—and it was unbearable to see her cry, but the doctors said it was a good sign; she left as soon as they stopped questioning her, her father, her brothers, the whole family. She left disgusted, broken, unable to keep thinking or trying to see what she had not seen and to smell the breath that had not blown in her face. She left thinking, it's true, about the unpolished wooden table, but above all about the distance, about how in the land of the great rivers there would be no police stations or medical examiners or nosiness or empty lots or photos of her sister in the place where the bloodied face had been.

Now that man that was her husband was waving to her, he didn't smile at her but he tried to and he was friendly. He didn't hold out his hand, either. He only said he was happy to see her and how was the journey? She said good, only that it was good, and was unable to stop looking at him. She had to know what this man was like and she had to know it soon; before, if it were possible, before she reached the house.

When they had come home from the hospital at night, late by then, her father, her mother, she and her two brothers had sat down around the table and she had felt she had to do something, anything except be there, silent, all trying not to look at each other.

"Shall I prepare tea?"

No one answered and, because she wanted to make tea and because she didn't want to remain seated across from the chair her sister always occupied, she got up and went to the kitchen and put the kettle on the burner.

She could not, much as she tried, could not imagine how it had been. She could not even think about what Bridget had felt on seeing the flash of the knife. Had she seen that? she asked herself again. The light on the sharp blade threatening her like a lifeless eye? Or first the shadow of the man who hurried ahead until he blocked her way and made her stop beside the ruined wall? The whistle of the kettle was like the *fzzzz* of the knife but no, he hadn't slashed her, not at that moment. She heated the teapot and put the kettle back on the stove, not on the burner but to one side so it would keep a low boil. Tea is made with boiling water, not boiled water, and the teapot has to be hot, and no putting cold water in it, because it's not true the boiling stream burns the tea leaves, and the stream one drizzles over the leaves that begin to open has to be soft because no, no, no pouring the water that comes out of the teakettle's spout in all at once, careful about that. Or maybe he had punched her when she resisted and only later, to kill her or so she would know he could kill her if he wanted to, only later had the slash arrived and now she was in the hospital with all those people dancing around her and smiling at her and putting tubes and needles into her all over.

She carried the teapot to the dining room and settled it carefully on the cork trivet. Osmán followed them, carrying the luggage which was not very abundant, a large suitcase, a smaller one, the typewriter box, and a traveling bag. Under that sun, in that heat, the tea would have to be served cold, very cold, in tall glasses and not in a clay teapot heated up and kept close to the burner. He asked if she played the piano. Yes, she said, she had learned as a child but she hadn't played for a long time, that's what she told him.

Bridget would get well, there was no doubt. She would begin little by little to practice, to try to learn all the everyday gestures again; with time, the nightmares would disappear, she would once more go to the cinema with her friends, she would be able to laugh at small events, she would make plans, she would talk on the telephone, she would buy new clothes, accept invitations to birthday parties, she would be once again as she was before, only far away from her. She would always carry the mark, the sketch of the knife wound on her shoulder as far as the clavicle; she would not be able to wear low-cut necklines or perhaps at some point it would no longer matter to her and she would wear whatever she pleased. She asked if there was a piano in the house and he said no but he had been thinking about bringing one, not an upright, something more resonant, more luxurious. A baby grand, perhaps, and that seemed fine to her, or at least that's what she said, that it seemed fine. The guy had run away and Bridget had been left lying in the empty lot, bleeding. If she had not been strong and determined, death would have fallen on her like a blanket. But she dragged herself to the street, moaning, covered in blood, and a few minutes later, someone saw her.

Her father took his tea without sugar and without milk, always. Her mother no, she liked tea with a drop of milk and the brothers drank it any old way. The house, she saw on rounding the bend, was not of marble and crystal but of wood. Unpolished wood, she hoped like that of some table she would be able to use for the typewriter, papers, envelopes, folders and, yes, if there were no bookcases, she could arrange to have them make her some shelves.

"This is your home now," he said.

She said thank you and then, it seemed with a certain effort, he smiled.

The Sense of Direction

HER BEDROOM WAS spacious. From a very strange room, without windows and so octagonal it was round—a room in which perhaps, if she were able to hear them, the voices of those who had called to one another there still echoed, or one might yet see, beneath a semitransparent, misleading tunic, the desperate or happy gestures of arms surrendering, legs trying to run, mouths that do not speak but smile; round, eight sides, or at least that's what she believed she saw the first day, and from there one climbed three steps to reach the bedroom. The window was in the opposite wall, across from the door. There was a small dressing room and a bath, all white. Almost a hotel room, she thought, she who had never been in a hotel except when she was very young at the beach with the whole family and they, the two girls, shared a hot room in which the two beds had flowered spreads, like the curtains. Here there were no curtains, the bed was large and the bedspread was white, with tassels that did not touch the floor on either side.

The morning passed in getting settled. Clothes, shoes, boots, tall boots he had told her to bring in the letter, belts, all that in the dressing room. Creams and powders and soaps in the bath. The typewriter, where would she put the typewriter? There was no table; chairs, yes, two, but no table. She did not take it out of its case and she slid it under the bed. She had not brought photographs; on the bedside table she put only a clock and the notebook and pencil.

Her movements were slow; for some reason, her movements were slow. She thought: *I am killing time so as not to find myself with him.* It could be so, or not, perhaps not, although yes, in part—but there was something more. Something that, hands on her hips, something she hid from herself and that she would have to, looking around her, she would have to use up by means of words she would say, would say to herself; that was it, tell herself in so many words. Or better, crumble it, reduce it to sandstone and that something was—what was it?

What had she been who was in fact another, not this person? What had been her dream of being alone and free? Only that wasn't all: it would have been easy if it were, there in the land of the great rivers, face to face with the man who is her husband and who will also, at night, wait for her, although not knives and possibly (yes) blood, who would claim her and she would not be able to resist and would not have anyone there who would dance around her, only the music of the piano, what an idea, a piano that did not exist, was not there, that he was planning to order.

Would the piano arrive on the same worn-out little boat that had brought her, wrapped in cotton padding so the polish wouldn't suffer, the keys covered with a soft cloth? She would not touch the keys of a piano, polonaises and Elise and Vienna and lieder; she no longer knew how. The keys of the typewriter wait for her, how could she not wish they might be waiting for her. She would set herself to hating him, hating him so that he would never force her to play the piano for him, seated beside the lamp, elbow on the table, hand cupped under his chin; he would listen smiling, as he had smiled a little while ago, with great effort, against the current of something that was not exactly the music but rather a hard bezoar made of days that make up a story, of hours that make up a life, of steps and doubts and above all echoes, the echoes that the water of the river awakens against the stilts of the jetty, echoes of brushes, of sterile nights with half-closed eyes taking refuge on the ceiling that grows lighter with the dawn, of music and syllables and tracks which will not be erased just like that by wishing. She would not extract melodies playing the absent keys of a nonexistent piano that would arrive—or perhaps not—by way of the river and the mud.

There was a secret route that went from his arrogance to her resentment, which she would not dare, she did not now dare, traverse. What would she say to him? How would she say it? It no longer resonated as an echo, but rather, yes, strictly speaking, certainly, as an alarm signaling the terror and disgust that had brought her to the wooden house beside the river. Deeper still, where the blood's hammer beats against the skull and at the borders of the eyes, the rumble of the muscles sings and sings and the air slides down along that hollow tree, deeper and deeper still, to where only at the moment of death or in madness are words given to what torments the belly and crosses the throat; there where she could not reach, which was the soul of the stone, of the pulp of her flesh, at that sleeping limit she had wanted to—since the Friday of the bloodied face in the newspaper, since long before, since long after when Bridget had dragged herself wounded to the street, since she was among the plump-legged girls—ever since then she had wanted to leave off being who she was and now, first as ink and today as presence, that it should be he, that man who would do it for her. So yes, she had to hate him, it was her obligation so that the one she had been would not cease to be.

If that had not happened, if Bridget had not been attacked, suffered the pain and the knifing, she would not be there, no: she would have continued in the house that resembled other houses on other streets, impatient, fleeing the yellow evenings, telling herself that one day she would sit down at a table to write about the absence, misunderstandings, the injustice, catastrophes and torments; about what people inflict on one another, about how it is possible to write. But Bridget stained with blood and tears had made it so she could no longer feel indifference and irritation toward the house. Starting that night, her family, the house, had a different consistency, to which she could not respond. What to do, what to say, how to make steps echo on the stairs, how to return from the supermarket to put the groceries in the kitchen while thinking of something else? How to address her mother, her father, without their guessing that, now that they mattered to her, she could not continue living with them? Either explain what she felt, make an inventory and a confession, or leave. Leave. Confess yes, but leave: what she had always wanted, to leave.

Osmán ate lunch with them. She didn't know if this was a custom or if it had occurred to him that day so everything, the conversation, the glances, might be easier. And everything was, in effect, easy as could be. The little man told her the history of

La Preciada, he explained what was done there, he spoke of the tribes, the desert, the forest that ran the length of the two banks of the river and he reviewed the house staff with whom, he believed, she would need to have contact.

What Osmán said interested her. She was thinking about what she would write, about the place she might or might not be able to find for the typewriter, but at the same time she listened to the history and the geography and the survey of personnel that Osmán shelled out. Perhaps the two things were one. No, of course not, she would never concern herself with those topics: a house, a business, a river, men and women of the forest and of the desert. But nevertheless she could not, just like that, give up the frame of witchcraft that adorned what Osmán was telling her. The tribes.

"All different," Osmán said, and her husband let him talk, "it depends, it seems to me, it depends on where it is they come from. Take for example those of the plains. Plainsmen, people call them, because it's easier that way, but their name is Chetvas, that's it, the tribe of the Chetvas. They're the most reliable."

Her husband, that man seated at her left, laughed.

"Don't you believe him," he said, and she was startled by his sudden use of the informal address, "not one of them is reliable. Not one of any tribe."

"You let me explain it to the lady," Osmán said softly, not as an objection or like someone starting an argument; smiling, even. "Because otherwise the lady is going to think she has come to live among savages, and it is not so, believe me, it is not so. They have their ways, I don't say they don't, but as soon as you begin to get to know them and follow their lead, everything happens more naturally, you will see."

Similarly docile, he, the owner of La Preciada, nodded as if in agreement and allowed the other man to continue.

"Now," Osmán went on, "there are the Halsas, who live in the forests. Forests, you will have noticed, forests there aren't many, but those there are grow on the banks of the rivers and they are impressive, hard and very dark. Such are the forests of the land of the rivers."

"Don't people live on the rivers?" she asked.

"No, ma'am, no. What's on the bottom is soft, and it's always changing when the river rises and with the currents. One can't set pilings on the bottom to build houses on top. And as far as living on boats, that really is dangerous, there's some of everything in the rivers. Near the rivers, yes, in the forests. They're good workers, the Halsas, not very strong, the damp of the river, you know? It doesn't agree with them. But they're skilled and they work as balers, just as those from the plains, the Chetvas, are collectors and gatherers. And after that come the nomads, who are the best workers and therefore they're contracted to pick everything up. They're strong, those fellows really are strong, they bump around with all kinds of trouble from one place to another looking for the best spots. True, they can be a problem. Not always, but they often seem to be looking for the hair in the milk, and they come with all kinds of complaints, sometimes so strange you don't know how to resolve them."

"What are they called? Just that, nomads?"

"Nooo, even there, they're complicated. They're called Abu'nakues, with an aspiration that isn't quite an h, between the u and the n."

At her left that man, her husband, he who had so suddenly addressed her informally, twisted the tip of a knife against the orange skin. She, his wife, who did not yet know how to address him, thought she would not meddle in the kitchen but that she would like to see the nomads, the Abu'nakues, those with an almost-h in the middle of their name, and to speak with the Chetvas, the plainsmen that Osmán said were the best of them. Best? Most tranquil, he clarified, most approachable.

Lunch was coming to an end, there was no more to say and she stood up.

"Osmán could take you," he said, "to get to know the place, show you where everything is. But you will have to put on your boots and cover your head. There's an infernal heat out there at this hour. Only if you want to go, of course."

"Yes, I want to," she said.

"I will wait for you in the gallery, ma'am."

"I'll go put on my boots and be right there."

He did not follow her; to her relief, he did not follow her. She walked to the small, almost round room without windows and he went in, she saw him, she didn't want to look, didn't want to turn her head, but she saw him from the corner of her eye going into the office.

Very Imperfect Reports

MUCH LATER, WHEN ominous news was arriving daily, when she was running La Preciada and had been adopted as *derba-nuru* by the Chetvas, much later she would ask herself how it all began. When she thought of that, of how it had been and who and why had put up a fight, she could remember only a few things. That she, for example, had discovered, left in a warehouse, under canvas and ropes and traps for small rodents, an unpolished wooden table and had told Osmán to have it carried to her room. Osmán, who seemed to be always at her disposal, called a pair of huge men (nomads, she learned later, but at the time they all looked the same to her) and had them carry the table inside. She remembered the difficulty they had getting the table through the narrow doorways into the antechamber and from there to the bedroom. All very well, but that had nothing to do with the fights and the arguments. He hadn't even known about the table that was now in her bedroom.

Two days after her arrival, a boat had docked and a kind of fury of work had been unleashed among the people of La Preciada, but that didn't help her, either. And there was the matter of the boots. He saw her leave the bedroom barefoot and was alarmed. "Please!" he yelled, "please, never go barefoot, indoors or out!" and once she had put something on her feet he took her down close to the river and he lifted the bark on the side of a stump and, terrified, she could see those nameless bugs, *curús* Tuca called them, amber yellow, almost transparent, that fled from the light and raised the stinger in which the black poison floated. He didn't even tell her what could happen if one of them bit her, she found that out later, but she never again walked barefoot, inside or outside the house.

What she did remember with complete clarity was that the days passed without her husband approaching her. Possibly he had observed that she was intrigued, relieved and intrigued, because one evening, sitting on the gallery, without looking at her, he had told her directly that he was waiting for her to become acclimated and above all to get to know him a little better, for their marriage to become a real one. She did not know what to say and all that came out was a "That seems very good to me," and a "Thank you" that afterward she considered completely out of place. But it was already said.

Now, how it happened that the quarrels began, the arguments and the fights, that she didn't remember. She believed—but to believe is neither to remember nor to know—she believed the first one had been not quite a fight and not even an argument, but certainly a rough conversation, at the top of their voices, because he had said, had repeated, that none of the men, none of the women of any of the tribes was trustworthy. They were all cunning, crafty, hypocrites, traitors, as well as being ignorant and stupid, and they didn't even try to learn to speak a civilized language.

She, she didn't know if always but at least since she'd had dealings with the police and the medical examiners and the lawyers and all that, she was on the side of the attacked. She had asked him if he had made an effort to learn the words that were used in each tribe. That seemed to him foolish and insolent, and she had been pleased. He said one has to be crazy to want to learn the language of monkeys and she told him she was going to learn because she thought it was crazier to communicate by signs and thus make mistakes at every step. He answered that for him the only important thing about those fellows was that they work and he didn't care a bit about the rest of it.

"Like animals," she said.

"Yes," he answered her, "like animals. That's what they are."

From that point forward, everything had been a continual fight, whatever it might be about, shouting at any hour, anywhere and in the presence of whoever might be nearby. It seemed, suddenly, that they could not speak to each other in a normal tone, it was impossible for one to address the other without shouting, without reproaching them for something, any little nonsense; impossible to look at one another, never mind smile, or exchange greetings, two words, a checkup, a gesture.

She was trapped. She said those words to herself and searched within for the anguish of feeling herself restrained, with no possibility of freeing herself from that ground, that river, that house, La Preciada, that man, and she found nothing that resembled the desolate captivity she imagined when she said to herself, "I am trapped." She was trapped but she felt satisfied. More than that, exultant, active as she had never been under the gray sky of the country where she had been born. She woke up before dawn and wrote until breakfast. The golden letters on the typewriter on the unpolished wooden table sparkled in the sun that came in through the curtainless window. What did it matter? The sun, that was the essential thing, the sun, more than the curtains. Nothing, ever, she was sure of that, nothing blossoms under a gray sky. The sun nourishes words, sketches scenes, sings verses and fills silences with projects and possibilities.

The novel was called *Uncertainty* and it had an epigraph from Muriel Spark: "Wonders never cease." It was the story of a woman who was writing a novel, but it wasn't about herself that she wrote, rather about a woman she did not know, whom she had never seen and who probably did not exist under any sky. But she went through the possible skies, she did, because she did not want to write the story of a young woman who has gone to live in the land of the great rivers but rather something else, something close by and unknown, the mystery, that shadowy word, that she could cover with words. Another language. Spain, she came to think. But no. A country where they sang the *danzón* and danced slowly. Perhaps Brazil, violent country of sun. Or an island in the tropics. When she could imagine, still without names, those streets and those parks and those evenings and that music on the map, she felt everything was in its place, in the space that belonged to it, settled. To write, only to write.

She was writing and she was writing the novel of the woman who was writing a novel and allowed the sun, the dark water of the river, the sounds of La Preciada to flood her. None of that mattered to her, nothing, not even the man. She had enough, and she put up a fight whenever she could, which was often. He seemed to be more furious every day. It was no longer a matter of the piano or of difficult conversations in the gallery. It was only a matter of writing early in the morning, and fighting at any other time.

"You are an imbecile!"

"You don't call me an imbecile, who do you think you are, you good-for-nothing lay-about."

"Your mother must have been a good-for-nothing, I imagine your grandmother, too. And I'll call you imbecile as much as I want, sir, because you deserve it, you hear me? You deserve it. If you could at least hear what the others say to you, you might think, if you're capable of thinking, that someone other than you might be right."

"The others? What are you saying? Yeah, I get it, what you're saying is I have to listen to you, right? Isn't that it? That's it, a newcomer who doesn't know anything about anything!"

"I haven't been here long and I already know much more than you."

"Will you shut up for once?"

"I'm not going to shut up because I don't want to!"

And so on for half an hour, ten minutes, an hour, whatever they could stand so as to cultivate their fury, make it grow.

But it wasn't just writing early in the morning and fighting all the time. It was also learning to talk to the people of the tribes, and that was something that made him so furious she felt something that could have been fear and began to try to speak with them when her husband—oh, yes, her husband even though he was not—was far away or was busy with something that would keep him away from her.

She remembered her first classes in Spanish and in German and decided to start that way. She tried it with the nomads but only got through the first basics. What escaped her was not always the meaning of the words she was learning but something else,

what was just behind the words, all that in which she had had
no part, had not seen, could not remember, demand, awaken;
the touch of the hides, the scent of the milk of the animals
they moved in droves, the moving a bit further away or a little
closer when water or food began to grow scarce or when the
boss decided it was time. With those of the forest it was easier
because they seemed interested in learning. They, the Halsas, were
taller than the Abu'nakues but also thinner, almost slender, and
they had shining, curious eyes, so that in a short time they could
exchange phrases and make themselves understood. It was her
first triumph. It wasn't very clear why or over what she had to
triumph but she felt triumphant that way, dismantling walls and
obstacles between herself and them.

Granted, it was the Chetvas with whom she could, after some
effort and a lot of laughter, but very quickly as she later understood, communicate almost fluidly; above all with the Chetva
women. They were not as tall as the nomads nor as slender as the
forest dwellers but they smiled a lot more than the others and the
women approached her and touched her blond hair and spoke
very quietly words that at first she had not understood and that
nevertheless, little by little, she finally made her own. They learned
I and *you* (they had a single form of the second person pronoun,
and it was almost, one might say, distanced and even ceremoni-
ous); they learned *house* and *let's go* and *sky* and how to distinguish
between *to eat* and *food* or *meal*. She, too, learned how those things
were said in the language Chetnai. They were the Chetvas and
the language they spoke was Chetnai and the plains or the desert,
which to them were a single thing, was the (feminine) Anetchetai.

They didn't get together among themselves. The nomads,
proud and hard, wanted nothing to do with the others. The
people of the forest, more apathetic, sometimes worked with the

plainsmen but without speaking to each other, and the Chetvas did not seem very interested. Osmán did seem interested in what she was doing but he never told her; it was something she guessed from a look, a way of sitting close to her when she taught the members of the tribes words, acting as if he neither saw nor heard her. It was a silent, quiet company; maybe it wouldn't serve for much, but he was there, without moving, until her husband called, looking for him. He'd stand up as if it cost him to start to walk and he'd go, without looking back.

Privilege

SHE LIVED AS if in two worlds at once. The two were concrete and demanding, without cracks, and the two weighed the same. She moved through the two over days that were weeks and were months and flowed into page 31 of the novel she was writing about that woman who writes a novel.

The woman, her name is Celina, is sixty-four years old and widowed. That is to say, she, Celina, believes she is a widow. She, the one who writes, knows she is not; she knows that twenty years ago her husband apparently died when the plane he was traveling in crashed. That was what Celina had always believed. But she knows he saved himself by swimming; he woke up in a hospital, wounded and without his memory. She knows his memory, his recollections, everything had come back slowly, day by day, and while there on the coast where the plane had crashed they tried to identify the few disfigured bodies—swollen, almost destroyed—that the sea returned day after day, he had decided there was nothing wrong with being dead, he preferred to disappear, to be someone else or to try to be someone else. Because, she has this written down in her notebook, because he and Celina had not had children, so there was nothing, no one, no family responsibilities that obliged him to live that wearying, narrow time, always so much the same, so much the same. He was fed up with the wearisome life he led day after day, no greater excitement or surprise than the visit of a brother-in-law, the voice of a friend or a colleague on the telephone, what there was for dinner, a gathering of boring intellectuals, sometimes the usual cinema to see movies he didn't like, the checked tablecloths, the waxed floors, locking the front door at night. He had never regretted it.

What that dead husband who was not dead did was just a mention in the novel. What mattered was Celina, the woman who writes a novel about a life that is exactly the same day after day, a life that all of a sudden explodes in a sea of confusion and reveals—what? The fragility of life, the misunderstandings, the small domestic details that are in fact catastrophes when one goes through them day after day until they become the sharp edge of an abyss, the moment at which an entire life turns and changes and it is no longer possible to go back. That is what she was doing, and she tried not to do anything other than that, than write. So much so that she overlooked what was happening in La Preciada, day after day.

If it had not been for Osmán, she would not have known. What would have happened, she asked herself, if she had not been informed? Probably nothing. Twenty-four hours, maybe forty-eight, no more, to notice he was not there. Or maybe she would have noticed on her own, because the preparations were quite telling and noisy. But yet again no, because she was living in the two worlds, in that of La Preciada and in that of *Uncertainty*, and beyond that, beyond the sun, the river, the desert, the house on one side and the woman who does not know that death will come so soon and who writes and remembers as if she were immortal, which she is—beyond that, everything was haze, shadow, veil, the opacity of a ghost against the light that entered through the window, under the lamp she lit at dawn.

"When the boss leaves," said Osmán, "in the week when he is not here, what do you think, ma'am, if we bring in some women, just the ones from the plains, so they can give the house a good cleaning?"

"He's going when?" she asked.

"Three days from now."

"Yes, well, it's not a bad idea. Leave it to me, I'll speak with them."

Osmán agreed and she glimpsed a week of silence and the smell of bleach; she told herself she was going to put flowers—where was she going to get flowers?—not flowers, then, branches of different shades of green in the dining room and the parlor. She thought, oddly, not about writing but about overseeing the housecleaning. *Curús* would probably appear in the corners or under the floorboards, so she would need to have the poison to hand but use it with care. It would be better if she or Osmán used it and not the plainswomen who seemed unaware that there were dangers besides those they already knew about: thirst, the big cats with their spotted tails, fire at midday, the *arurays*, those whitish snakes that disappear against the sand, the *cuaimas*, stomach upset, wounds, those who died of shame or cowardice, those who returned on stormy nights trying to repair what they had done or what they had not done and who avenged themselves of their eternal punishment on those who were still living, those who, still alive, saw the light, ate *escallia* leaves dunked in a broth of bread and pork, walked and sang and went into the river and had meat on their bones and blood in their arms and fertile juices in their kidneys. She would have to take care of the world of those Chetva women who barely brushed the world that belonged to her, to which she belonged, and that was silently cracking behind their backs. They should be wary of the dark and humid corners, they should not approach carelessly, but they should not be the ones to use the poison against the amber-yellow insects.

He would go with five men, three Abu'nakues and two plainsmen to carry the provisions, weapons, tents, clothing, water, everything needed to cross the desert, toward the interior, not toward the river. To do what, she wasn't sure. She heard talk of seeds and also of contracts; expired contracts, he said in the dining room, he said it to Osmán and she heard and that was enough for her. He would go for a week, for something, to do or to look for something, a week in which she would write, she would walk down to the jetty to see the water sparkle, she would talk with the Chetva women, she would put green branches in the dining room every day of that week.

He did not say he was leaving. Three days later, as Osmán had said, they ran into each other in the eight-sided anteroom, and then yes, at that moment he said to her, I'm leaving and she said, I'm glad.

"Oh yes?" he said.

"Yes, I'm glad, I'm glad you're going, because I hate you, did you hear me? I hate you."

"I heard you, but you are not going to have much time to hate because as soon as I return, I am going to throw you out of here."

He said it calmly, without shouting; he said it and he left.

Epic Song

IT WAS A week of sun and silence. It wasn't that the sun always shone, given that there were gray days or foggy ones; it wasn't that no one spoke or that they didn't make noise. There was all that, just as always, everything she was accustomed to seeing and hearing in La Preciada. But she wrote not only early in the morning but also after lunch and in the evening and sometimes at night, too. Little by little, uncertain and slow, the woman in her novel began to appear, carefully, whenever she called her, obedient to the pressure of fingers on keys turned golden with the first sun.

And in the other world, too. In the other world, less demanding, there were fog and noises and voices and sun and she took part in all of it. Why wouldn't she? Why not, being lady and mistress? She was that when she sat down at the unpolished wooden table and put another sheet of paper in the typewriter. But she was also that, and she did not know it yet, when Osmán called on her to decide something.

"Do we put the whole load in the *Ocolocha*? I ask because there it comes, around the northern curve, see? You can hear the whistle, two blasts to announce it's coming, a pause, two more to announce it's docking, and we have to decide what to do."

"And why wouldn't you put in the whole load?"

Osmán explained. They kept back a third of the bundles in the large warehouse. ("We're very sorry but as the boss isn't here, it wasn't possible to complete the baling.") They would cause a shortage, not very great but noticeable, and from Pearl they'd send word that they needed more and in La Preciada they would act as if it wasn't possible until they offered to pay more than what they always paid.

"That does not seem right to me," she said.

"But, ma'am, it's done all the time. Everyone knows and plays along. They'll end up paying more."

"La Preciada is not going to fall into that," she said, lady and mistress.

Or else they had been left without anyone to gather up the rest of the load, damn nomads who disappeared whenever they were most needed.

"Let's talk to the Halsas and the Chetvas," she suggested.

"They won't want to, ma'am, I know what I'm talking about."

The Halsas weaseled out but the Chetvas, their women, said yes, as long as, looking down, as long as a few things they needed, and the sentence stopped there.

"What things do you need?" she asked.

They told her and she said fine, they would have hard floors, not tamped earth, and it would be arranged that a door be brought from Wanstown.

"Two," they said, "one for the front and one for the back."

"Like your big house," said one of the women.

Osmán looked at her and said nothing.

"That's fine, I promise," —to say *I promise* is a serious thing in Chetnai— "but you have to start today."

And when the Halsas found out the plainsmen were going to do the work, they said they, too, could do the work the nomads did, and they didn't ask for anything. She had said *I promise*, and she promised herself she would make good. When he arrived he was going to throw her out, but before that she would acquire— what? Tiles, stones, bricks for the floor and two doors like in the big house.

Lady and mistress, she began to look after La Preciada in the moments when she wasn't writing. For four days at least, maybe five and on the next day—no, the next, on the day after next—he would arrive and she would pack her bags and she wouldn't be able to take the unpolished wooden table but the typewriter, yes, and she would be happy knowing that a piano was never going to arrive in a worn-out little boat and he would never hear any music, sitting at the table, half-closing his eyes, hand under his chin. Two days, two and a half. But she would not pack her bags, she would not go before he arrived, she would not go without a final battle. And afterward, yes; after that, yes.

Reverberation

ONE DAY, ANOTHER, one more. At the end of the third, in the kitchen, Tuca said to her, "What do I do with this?"

"This" was a pig's intestine filled with a paste made of *zyminia* leaves and roots, flour, donkey's milk, eggs, and spicy seasoning. *Gasgos*, Tuca called it and he, her husband, loved it, that's why Tuca made it on special occasions. The return from that trip was a special occasion.

She asked Osmán if the owner of La Preciada was often delayed, arriving long after he said he would.

"No," said Osmán, very serious, shaking his head, "no, he always arrives when he says he is going to arrive." She didn't say anything and after a few seconds, uncomfortable, he continued, "He must have been delayed for a reason."

"Yes, of course," she said.

"Something, I don't say serious, but something he had to wait for. Possibly Svensson wasn't there and then, of course, you understand, no? He couldn't renew those contracts and then he'd surely have to wait for him."

"Ah."

She told Tuca to throw the *gasgos* in the garbage, that the master, lord and master, was not going to arrive that day.

"Should I make them tomorrow?"

"No," she said.

One week later, Osmán tried not to run into her and if he could not avoid it, he remained quiet, lowered his gaze and opened and closed his hands; he stood on one foot and then the other and finally went away, saying he had to do something urgent or else without saying anything. She, meanwhile, took care of La Preciada.

Two weeks later—two weeks busy with the arrival of boats, with gathering delayed by the rains, returning nomads, an unexpected roundup, balers who had to be convinced to work more hours than usual, loads, papers, remittances addressed with Osmán in the large office—two weeks later a canoe arrived with three men aboard and docked alongside the jetty. Tuca gave them coffee and rolls and they asked for water. They arrived tired, they said, they had been delayed and had been left without water because the river water, unfiltered—well, you know, better not drink it unless it's a question of life or death, and even then, why risk it? After the coffee and the water and the rolls and the commentary, they asked to speak to Osmán.

"Better you should tell her, don Osmán," one of them said, the one who took the lead, the one who had talked about the river water and being tired, about the eddies and the oars, "you tell her because one doesn't know, all of a sudden like that, what she is going to say and the truth is we didn't see anything, we weren't there. We know what we were told, that's all."

When the three men left in the canoe, toward the west, taking with them a barrel of water, fruit, and two fresh loaves, Osmán went to look for her.

"Ma'am," he said.

She lifted her eyes from the papers she was reviewing and when she saw his face, she stood up.

"What happened?" she said.

"They ambushed them, that's what the men said." Osmán didn't know where to begin and that's why he had done it so clumsily, with the first words that came to him.

But while he had thought, how do I tell her? where do I begin?, it never occurred to him she was going to guess everything before he could decide how to say what he had to say.

"Is he dead?"

"Aaah, yes . . . and the men, too."

At that moment, the first thing she thought was, And now? What am I going to do now?

"some recollection, circumscribed and waning"

SHE WOULD WAIT. Every day, because each day would bring something new and she simply needed to wait. Two letters had arrived from her home, short, staggered, no surprises. Bridget was better. She had returned home and the next week she would return to her job. Everyone—she didn't know who everyone was—had treated her very well. Her father was well, her mother had had a cold but had recovered. Her brothers sent their love, cousin Helen had had a baby, Madge Curtis' father had died of a syncope, and a bookstore with a lending library had opened three blocks from their house. She would wait for other letters, she would wait for news, she would wait for someone to come and tell her what had become of them, what the ambush had been like, how they had died, where, why.

The wait was made of time and time of wood and water; in the mornings it was made of papers, signatures, seals, and money put away in the strongbox. She told Osmán that was dangerous, in future he would have to take the raft once a week to deposit money in the bank. He said the boss didn't want the money to leave the house and she answered that the boss wasn't there anymore and she was in charge now. And with that, in saying that the man who was her husband would not return, the wait became something else, something she could not yet put a name to. She did not try; she only began to live in a different way, to do things she had not done when he was lord and master of La Preciada. She got up as early as before and wrote, as before, until breakfast. But the woman in *Uncertainty* cringed fearfully, she crouched in the corners and no longer looked her in the face, she no longer appeared, stubborn and silent, so that she could write her, and sometimes she moved further away until she disappeared and, writing, she started putting on the sheet of paper other characters that called to the woman. Or no, that did not call her and did not speak to her, that only walked or drank or spoke and laughed or ate or climbed stone steps hoping, they too, that the woman of the novel would come back and look at her.

And she moved through the house as she had not done before, not even when he had said, "This is your home now." She hired two women from the plains to clean, wash the clothes, serve at table. She had to convince both the women and the men of the families because the Chetvas thought it was fine that the men should work outside the tribe, and also that the women should work, but within the tribe, not in the big house. There were days of conversations, proposals, denials, temptations, everything that was within her reach until the women came over to her side and the men gave in. She had thought Tuca would resist having other women in the house doing the cleaning and washing, but the old woman felt these women also came to serve her and she received them with pleasure and even learned to make *mnagui* (she said it *munagüi*), a soup of yellow kernels in a thick broth scented with herbs that was one of the customary dishes at Chetva meals.

She had brought from Wanstown the stones for the floor and the two doors for the shack. She had promised, hadn't she, and a promise is meant to be kept. It seemed to her that from then onward the plainsmen looked at her differently, more respectfully, more distant. They smiled at her less but they approached and awaited orders until she, lady and mistress, decided what had to be done each day.

She put green branches in the dining room and in the parlor and that had an unexpected consequence.

"I'll bring the branches, if you like," said one of the plainswomen.

"Of course," she said.

And the woman brought flowers. She wanted to know where those orange and white corollas with a black or crimson center had come from and the woman, Savta she said her name was when she was hired, told her the tribe had them. From then on she always brought flowers for the dining room and the parlor.

She was still waiting, she was waiting for news of those who had left. She was waiting, she knew very dimly, hoping the bodies would be brought, she waited to bury that hated man, close to the river, on the edge of the forest so neither high water nor storms would reach it. Reports arrived instead, versions that contradicted each other: it had been the *morcós*, the ghosts of those who died by lightning, enraged because the six men had set foot on their territory and it's well known the *morcós* carry off not only the souls but also the bodies of those they kill. No, it had been bandits, robbing them; guys who travel the plains seeing what they can find to sell and with the money buy liquor and women in the *sirgal,* the prostitutes' quarter in Wanstown. But no, they had fallen into a jaguar trap and died at the bottom of hunger and thirst. They drowned in a backwater of the Malima. As so often when the men drew their two weeks' pay, a fight had broken out in a gambling den, and some great hulking guys from the south who no one seemed to know had started firing shots. All of this was an appeal to the sun, to the forests, to the danger-ous waters of the river; all, all of it when the light marked the outlines of objects and of people, when voices and tapping and calls could be heard, when the hours of the day were measured by smells from the kitchen, when one heard the gurgle of the water pump, the screech of the birds in the forest, footsteps, orders. It was different at night.

At night, unless there was a roundup (but the roundups had not been repeated), during the nights everything diminished, voices, noises, lights, even the flames in Tuca's ovens and the water of the river slapping against the dock pilings, the footsteps, the wind, the whistle of the *orcoles* with their grayish feathers and yellow crest, the hissing of the bales dragged by the Abu'nakues, the calls of the carrion-eaters, the rooting around of short-legged animals that came out to hunt snakes and desert rats, everything that during the day had had a voice, shout, murmur, whistle, everything.

She wrote at those moments. By the light of the lamp she put words to the woman of her novel or to those who surrounded her, awaiting her as she did—not Celina, but rather she who waited for that man, now dead, now no one, now a shadow like the husband of the woman in her novel who was not dead although

Celina might believe he was. Afterward, when she was too sleepy to keep writing, she went out through the octagonal anteroom and in the parlor she picked up another lamp and went through the house seeing that everything was in order. Room by room, the bars on the doors, the windows, the laundered clothing in the baskets, the table set for the next day's breakfast, pencils, pens, ink, blotting paper and forms to work on with Osmán until midday. Before going to bed she went through the bedroom of the dead man and she paused in that cold order of closed wardrobes, ironed bedspread, lamps without light, closed window. She went to her room, she undressed, she lay down and slept. But something stayed with her of that somber tour, something like retaliation, like saying you will never see La Preciada again, never again do anything here, never again dream of a piano, but I am alive, I give the orders, deposit the money in the bank, I put flowers in the dining room, I have dark-haired servants who adorn themselves with necklaces of colored beads. You are dead, you no longer give orders, you no longer eat *gasgos*, you don't yell obscenities at the harvesters and those who carry everything away after them, you don't grumble at Tuca and I hope stray dogs have eaten your corpse. Then he, as if answering, appeared to her, now on the verge of sleep, returning to La Preciada just as she had seen him on the day he had sworn he would throw her out when he returned. And so he returned; sleepily, she saw him return, enter the house and look at her without speaking and vanish only when sleep rocked her in a bed of clouds, in the deep silence of the heavens.

She slept and did not dream.

During the day she retained nothing of the visions of the night, nothing. Not fear nor pity nor rage. Only the sensation of having lifted an enormous weight, as the porters did with the bales, a certain tension in the flesh of shoulders and hips, those parts of the body that scaffold movement. And nonetheless, her feet were light, her hands flew over the typewriter or across the lists of numbers, she sat down comfortably, laughed, ate, inspected the cargo at the jetty, and had it not been for the shadow of a tightness in the center of her chest, here, below the throat, that she attributed to the responsibilities and the preoccupation with everything that had to be done during the day and on the next day and the day after that, she might have said she felt perfectly calm and happy.

Lodged perhaps in the nerves surrounding her pupils, the vision repeated itself at night. To conjure it, she sometimes encouraged it to appear in daylight. Then, leaning on the railing of the jetty or sitting in the shade of the gallery, she saw him enter the fields of La Preciada and spite made her clench her jaws until her ears hurt. What was that hated man doing there? How did he dare to return? What did he demand of her? And the pain in her chest and in her belly made her confess that she had called him.

She went to bed later every day, she got up earlier every morning, she wrote during the shadowy hours before the sun came up, she worked with Osmán in the office, with the plainsmen and those from the forest and the nomads on the jetty and in the shacks and in the warehouses, she inspected the women's tasks in the house and stopped by the kitchen so that old Tuca might tell her what she was making and what she needed; she often ate hurriedly, standing up, and planned strategies and designed time-tables and a different vessel every time Osmán went to deposit the money in the bank. When she grew used to being overcome by weariness, the visions disappeared.

I'm glad, she told herself, better that I don't see him anymore. I am never going to see him again, never. Nor am I going to bury him, but so what, it's not my obligation, it never was. Neither alive nor dead. I don't want to see him again walking toward me, ready to yell at me, to try to defeat me, hold my gaze, wipe out everything I am, submerge me in himself, in his will, in his cruelty, his hands must be like pincers coming out of those arms he imagines can encompass everything, people and animals and river and trees, against that knobby body, hard as steel, that now I am never going to see again. I'm glad. I only regret not having seen him die. I am never going to see him again. I'm glad.

Whether she liked it or not, he had remained in La Preciada. The shadow that enveloped her, the blood that had fallen drop by drop in the gambling den or the jaguar trap, the urgent voice, the steps she waited for and feared, *crrac crrac* of boots on sandy ground, the noises of the night or those of dawn in the bedroom next door, all of that was there even when she no longer saw it and was happy not to see it. She had, in her skin and in her hair, everything that the wind gathered and sometimes, when the air came most tangled, especially from the west, she left the house or the warehouse and walked out to that pale border that marked the beginning of the desert and she offered her face to the hot breeze that, obeying, slid over her as if with hands and feet and waist under her shirt collar and climbed up the back of her neck, pleased to be able to make her feel the power of the man who was no longer there. I'm glad, she said, I'm glad, and she straightened up so that she, too, could feel the weight of the power that from then on would assist her, alone and free as she had always wanted. And under the skin, taut and certain of its part in her defense, the reddened flesh of her muscles and the glacial and undecipherable distillate of her jaws resolved themselves in that determination to remain where she was, in what was from that day forward really her home; and where, when she turned her eyes to the water of the river or toward the forest, the barefoot path pointing toward the tribe, everything, each one of the ridges, summoned him only so that she might reject him and remember that, had he returned, he would have thrown her out, sent her on a journey toward the delta in the worn-out little boat, the ferry to reach Wanstown, the hydroplane destined for the gray city to which no, she would never return, just as now she would never again see him, and she was glad; she was glad even about the shadow and the drops of blood in the trap or in the ambush that were turning black on the ground. As if that blood fell on her breast and there became stone, or metal, or a knot impossible to untie, hard, stubborn, diamond-like.

Emergence

BUT AT TIMES. At times she felt she was not, herself, not entirely within her body, her own body, her limits of flesh and of humors, ashes promised to the final shadow. Then she forced herself into some physical task, an effort, something that would give her hands and her leg muscles something to do, something to feel the rush of her blood; or she made herself sleep. A little bit of sleepiness, just barely, drooping eyelids, one arm under the sofa cushion, or under the pillow on the bed, the other folded, hand supporting the opposite shoulder, comfortable. Ten minutes, she thought, and those were ten minutes of darkness, of distraction.

It wasn't hard for her to sleep. It hadn't been in the city, and it wasn't in the land of the great rivers. Celina claimed her sometimes and it was then she paid no attention to her hands or her eyelids. She went, she just went, as if to the future, as if to the rescue, and she sat down at the unpolished wooden table and no longer heard the noises of the house, the breath of the kitchen, the races around the water pump, that which all together was the heart of the ground under her feet, the disordered throbbing of La Preciada. Only one time, only once did she have trouble falling asleep and that was because she had had to mediate in a conflict among the men who wrapped the bales. To sleep. To sleep without dreams the way she slept, to straighten the sails of the shallow-bellied ships, take up the pace of the lizards over the sand, count words, let herself be, minimal chasm, scarcely buried, immobile, in a time one is finally able to leave outside of oneself, like a sour wine.

She knew Osmán would call her if something happened out there and she slept without dreams, protected and distant.

Around the house, many things might have been happening: the blond sand is never a fully inert mineral, the *curús* writhe in the damp cracks under the wood; the deceptive wind carries the scent of guano, of rotten fruits fallen from the trees, of bodies grateful to the shade that dries their sweat, of *multiflora* leaves, of peat, of the fury of a swift animal that throws itself onto its prey; the water roiled, trying to change course, and she slept, far from all that, unaware, pure. Dreaming is like a leap, it passes over events unharmed, wrapped in that germinal sac that is its own silence; and when it is about to fall at last on the other side of the chasm, there it is awaited by characters and events, words constructed of disparate letters, syllables that do not correspond to one another, one face instead of the other, and above all the absence of paths. What happens when one is in a place, but not the expected place or, worse, not the one which should inevitably follow after what had happened? What happens when it is a cave and not a staircase, when the person who speaks to one, dark, possessive, is not who it should be? She turned over uneasily because she would never, ever answer those questions she had not asked. Once and again, on her side, face down, face up, legs stretched out, no: knees toward the ceiling, once again on her side, because the throb of La Preciada had gotten into her dream. Osmán, it is true, would know what to do if something, something that demanded a solution, happened between the river and the desert. Osmán came and went in the dream of sleeplessness, her dream, her own dream without dreams, without silent, padded stages on which a bed becomes the screeching machine that in the bilge smells of sulfur and burnt oil, boards on which the litany of a scale sounds again and again. The piano, the dream told her, her very own dream, hers and no one else's, even as it slipped away from her, rebellious, every time and then another time as if calling her. Osmán did not defend her there: she herself, because she did not want to surrender, pavanes, Für Elise, minuets, she rebelled against the call and she moved in the bed, trying to escape. Asleep, entirely asleep, victim and protagonist, she allowed something more, the plot of the play, to insert itself on the threshold of whatever separates hard awareness—more even than alert, vigilant—from those secret, undesirable worlds that wait in the semidarkness a second before sleep, before waking, knowing one can't get out of bed barefoot, one must attend by force, oblige to silence.

The piano, she thought, it is useless to try to convince me, she thought. I am not going to play the piano for him. She sat up in bed. I have not seen him all day, she thought, he did not come to lunch. She stood up. I have to tell him this cannot be, she thought. She crossed the almost round antechamber and opened the door to the living room. And in front of her, when she saw further away the open door that gave onto the gallery, with the light, the sun almost white against the earth, the noise of the river that never stopped, she knew she had come out of the bedroom in search of a dead man. He was, she told herself with the light crossing the space until it reached her eyes, he was dead in the forest of Naruma or in the jaguar trap and he would not come back. No, he wasn't there. She and La Preciada continued to exist without him. Everything, everything that surrounded her had been left submerged in the dead man's absence. There was no piano on which might sound a pavane, a barcarole; now there never would be. He had died far away and she, carrying her dream on her back, looked for him—how was it possible?—in a watery world that little by little turned to mud and solidified around her.

The Hydra

"SAVTA," SHE SAID, "in addition to flowers, you need to bring seeds. Seeds, what one buries in the ground so another plant will grow."

The woman bent over and picked up something hard and blackish off the floor and showed it to her, as if she wanted to give it to her. It wasn't a seed; maybe it was a little bit of charcoal, or of rotten bark, or the remains of an insect, dry and hardened.

"That's it," she said, "the next time, seeds, all right? Seeds so flowers will grow."

In her country, city, street, house, in the little garden in front of the house, there had grown plants that blossomed in spring and in summer. No one took much care of them, not she nor her mother nor Bridget, never mind the brothers, but they blossomed. Nonetheless, she did not ask herself if this longing for blossoming plants was or was not a means of returning to the house to which never, but never ever, would she return. She simply wanted flowers, by the foundation of this house, "this is your home now," that house, the one of boards and the *curús* and the boat whistles and the canoes and the sun and the closeness of the desert.

"Ma'am," said Osmán.

"Yes, I heard it. It must be at the curve. Go and see if everything is ready. Don't forget to order the canvas."

There was something like a look of recognition, something that wasn't fully a change of expression and was like a stumble in the day-to-day crackle of eating and sleeping and speaking. She did not see it; Osmán almost did not even feel the ribbing of the uneasiness, but what was it he had said about the canvas to the other one, to the boss? When? The boat whistled again, this time close to the eddy they called Del Rumbo.

An hour later Osmán counted out loud the last bale that the nomads, barefoot and sweaty, carried up the landing stage.

"And twelve. Take this, it's your receipt."

"Osmán, have them sign the receipt."

"But ma'am, they don't know how to write."

"Look for someone aboard who does."

"Yes, ma'am."

Too much protocol, too much detail, although it could be that she was right, that it was necessary to verify every delivery, every bale, every rope, every footstep, every word.

Another hour later found her arguing in the warehouse shack with the Halsas who refused to work alongside the Abu'nakues. They took away their work, they tried to tell her; they were quick to steal, they said, and they stole their jobs.

"But I," she said, very slowly and supporting her words with gestures, "do not pay you for tasks completed but for hours you spend working."

"Flour," one of the men from the forest said quite clearly.

"Flour? You want flour instead of grain?"

"That's it."

There would be a party, she managed to understand. A celebration of something and they needed flour for the ritual meal. She told them yes, she would give them flour instead of grain, but with the same weight as the grain and they seemed to be in agreement. What kind of party might it be, she thought. And also thought that when the moon changed it would be the moment not for a party but for a family gathering, but within what she already knew was the great family of the Chetvas, the ones who had adopted her as *derba-nuru*, and that would be better than a party. An entire night barefoot at last because in the ground crossed by so many footsteps over so many days and nights there were no *curús*, dressed only in the yellow skirt of the Chetva women, a whole night of sitting among the women close to the fire, of hearing low, rapid voices murmuring over the water words like a chant, fearful words, protective words surrounding the animals, and the ceremonies of colors like feathers, a whole night of answering wisely if they asked her advice, of seeing the women nodding agreement when she spoke, of gathering with her fingers the sweet made of thistle and honey from the bottom of the bowls, of laughing and greeting and keeping silent with those who said, they said it, that they were her people.

But for the moment it was a matter of the flour that should weigh as much as the grain weighed, it was a matter of signed receipts and of gathering the necessary workers for the next load.

"When does the next one come?" she asked.

"Three weeks, ma'am," said Osmán, "now that we're in the dry season."

"They're all dry," she said, "if it weren't for the river and those storms that last less than a sigh, we would all be skin and bones."

Osmán smiled and told her not to forget that sometimes the rain fell without a break, mute and stubborn, dark, as if emerging from punishment down there below in hell, until it inundated all the land and licked at the base of the house. He didn't say it that way; he only said, "Sometimes it rains, don't forget, it rains with that dark rain that doesn't lift from one moment to the next."

The other bit, that was her thinking, as if the water that had fallen imposed itself upon her and prevented her from seeing any further, even the bank of the river.

"Yes," she said, "it happens sometimes, I know."

And the deep shadow of an unhappiness pierced her and took from her in an instant all reflection, it left her hollow, skin and bones, lady and mistress, day after day attending to the progress of La Preciada as if she were never again going to do anything other than take care of the cargo, the receipts, and the whistle of the boats coming lazily, with men on board smelling of liquor and tobacco, from an unknown spring: marsh surfaces shot through with the colors of putrefaction, trickles of water, a jump among the rocks; nothing that might announce the fact that far, far away, very far away there flowed one of those great rivers, a breath of water in six words of a letter written by hand, very neat, impersonal and not for that reason any less decisive.

Dirge

WHEN THE LAST bale was on the filthy deck of the *Lady R.*, when she knew it could rain or not rain or thunder or hail or the earth could sink into the river, it didn't matter anymore, she told herself she would leave both men and animals at liberty for a week, not longer, and afterward, only after those seven days, would she begin with the next load. She wanted to return to the woman, Celina, lying on the white bed, thinking about death. She wanted to keep writing about unspeakable secrets, injustice, catastrophes, the torments of time, the sowing of sorrow, silence.

The *Lady R.* whistled once more by way of farewell and moved away from the dock. It had come from up there, from where the river was just a hint of hidden water about to burst against the earth; it was going toward the south, heavy with cargo, slow and almost stately in spite of the rust and the dirty grease smears on the remnants of white paint.

"Go on," she said as if the boat could hear her, "and don't come back." They should send another one, more reliable, three weeks from now.

But she did not go sit down at the table. She did not put another sheet in the typewriter. She did not take notes or correct paragraphs. In the kitchen, she drank sugared coffee and two glasses of water.

"Osmán," she said when the little man appeared in the kitchen, "find Savta and her sister for me and tell them we need to put things in order. I leave the office to you, separate the receipts and put away what you can and close the cupboard and the box. I will wait for them in the parlor."

Two hours later, the sun high and ferocious but the women in the cool shade inside the house, they replaced the white dishes on the shelves, so clean they almost shone in the dark air of the dining room. I'm tired, she thought, I would do better to lie down for a while, eat something and lie down and then see—write, yes, but first try to rest.

"Help me roll out the carpet."

Savta's older sister, taller and stronger, told her to leave it for her; she could do it, she said, she should leave it to her because she already knew where the carpet went.

"It's heavy," she said.

Outside, very far away it seemed, outside, someone was yelling.

"I can do it, you'll see," said Savta's sister.

Shouting, people running, something was happening, something that was not another boat looking for another cargo, it couldn't be.

"What's happening out there?"

The two sisters were quiet. The older one let go of the carpet and straightened up, Savta twisted her head like a bird, trying to hear what was coming closer all the time.

"I'm going to see," she said.

She crossed the dining room and the parlor, went out to the gallery. Everyone, men and women and Tuca and Osmán and little kids coming out of the Chetvas' shack seemed to be waiting for something or someone, and toward the west, one could see that something, a dust cloud, a tumult, men coming toward the house. Osmán ran up to her as soon as he saw her. "It's him, it's him! He's come back, he's come back!"

A woman cried out (it seemed she was right beside her ear) that the dead were returning from the tomb of the jaguar; of the jaguar, of the jaguar the woman said, covered with blood, she said, they're coming. She believed the woman, and she believed her because it could not be otherwise. A *derba-nuru*, yellow skirt, hair gathered at the nape of her neck sitting barefoot before the fire in the murmur of the nights, the voices, the rhythm, a *derba-nuru* knows all that because she has proven that she knows the soul and the words of her people, and she understood that it could not be but it was, it was impossible but it was true; that he lay, a corpse almost devoured by stray dogs, skin and bones, unrecognized and stiff, gnawed, sleeping, without eyes, hair, now gray, almost invisible against the dirt, the bones of the fingers in the air naked at the bottom of the trap or under the floorboards of the gambling den or at the foot a tree in the forest of Naruma or skinned by the ants in the desert. It can't be that he returns alive, once again alive and hands like pincers voice of command dreams of a piano and sounds of footsteps in the bedroom next to hers, he is dead in the trap, it can't be, or dry, brittle under the desert sun while the woman kept yelling, more like a sob all the time, that the dead were returning and in spite of the visions or her desire she believed her, it was true, he was coming back.

The shouting and exclamations and the feet drumming on the ground were stronger all the time and she thought once again, as she had before, And now? What am I going to do now?

About Face

HE SAW HER arrive; he saw how she came running, came toward him, like that, running, out of the dark house of dark wood, green base, colors he did not understand, she came running toward him and he opened his arms running and arriving and clasped her against him, knobby, dry, hard as steel, and they kept walking.

A long path, that one, on the fine, rebellious dirt, almost sand, that rose up and settled back again at every step, a long way to the house. He heard as if without wanting to; he heard as he passed close to the groups that waited and talked, about how he had come back, about how in fact he had not died, or maybe he had, about how it was impossible to know, about how two of the men who had gone with him were missing, about how the spirits of the dead had kept them as security.

He smelled of dried blood; he smelled the way wounded animals smell when someone approaches to finish them off. He smelled of hard leather staked out in the sun, but not of death, no, not of death.

Tuca waited in the doorway of the house, eyes wide with fear or surprise, hands crossed over her belly and her lips just barely separated as if to ask, but without bringing herself to ask. She came in clinging to the man, he came in supporting her and she said to Savta, who was waiting, carpet forgotten, "Hot water, run the water until it comes out good and hot and prepare a bath and, oh, Tuca, thick beef broth, and cold cloths, he seems feverish."

He detached her gently, taking her by the hands, without looking at her yet, and he took off his shirt and went slowly toward the bathroom where he sat down to take off his boots. Careful, she thought, remembering the *curús*, but she knew he knew and moreover she saw him remain still, waiting, without touching the floor with his reddened feet which hurt, she thought, they hurt him, wounded and hardened, eaten away by sand and sweat. Tuca came and behind her two men who were waiting and Tuca went into the bathroom and opened the taps and covered the drain. The water bubbled, steaming, and he remained seated looking at his bare feet. She moved away after having looked in again, perhaps to assure herself that he was alive and the stains on his clothes were not jaguars' blood or bite marks from the *morcós*.

"Tuca," she was already leaving when she saw her come out of the bathroom, "Tuca, let him bathe in peace but don't close the door all the way and have one of the men stay close by in case the boss needs something."

Of course, said Tuca, who already seemed to have left surprise behind, and terror, too, before the certainty that it was a walking dead man. Of course, and she was going to heat up the broth.

She didn't ask herself, And now, what am I going to do now? She went to look for Savta's sister to finish putting the front room in order. The carpet, where had the carpet gotten to? Savta's sister, who was so tall and so strong, had put it in its place and she, lady and mistress, for the moment had nothing to do other than wait for him to come and tell her to leave.

Only he didn't come. He called to ask for clean clothes. Clean clothes, how had she not remembered clean clothes, how?

Afterward he passed close—not too close—to where she was, and told her he needed to sleep.

Nor had she thought of that, the sleep he was doubtless lacking, on guard all those nights scanning for danger, lighting dry branches, making the green branches smoke, torches to reveal vipers if there were any; walking by day, hiding from she did not know whom or what, but looking for shelter, coming out into the sun again, reached by claws or lances, eyes open always open to keep living and return.

Return, he was trying to return, that was it, why did he have to return? Return and tell her to leave. He had come back for that, she was sure. But she would not go, no, she would not go, and the shadow of the tightness at the base of her throat became the echo, the wound through which her life passed without consolation. All that she had lived would never be repeated and there ahead the afternoon shadow of the walls waited for her lit by the reflection of the *derba-nuru*'s yellow skirt. She could go live with her people in the village of the Chetvas; stay there, not go only when they called her but stay there, live among them, help the women when they gave birth, like that time, the evening when the women had told her she would be one of theirs, that to have saved a sister was sufficient qualification, because the life of one of them was the life of all the women and she had not understood much, she had not known at the beginning what it was all about. She had only run when she heard the cries and had attended the woman at the door of the shack, why not, with what she knew of first aid, what she'd learned in her schooldays when between grammar and history someone came to give a lesson on a faceless doll. And later, only later, her hands red with blood and her pulse racing, only then did she manage to evoke Bridget—who had not died in the vacant lot because someone had seen her drag herself toward the street—and make the leap from her to this other woman who had not died giving birth at the door to the shack because she at some point had learned something about how to attend a woman in labor. If she was a Chetva because of being a *derba-nuru*, which was better than just being a woman born and raised in the village, why not stay to live with them? When she went—why not go? She would not have to take anything, anything with her, not even clogs.

And at that moment he came out of the bath, white pants and clogs, and looked at her.

"Sleep," he said, "I'm going to sleep. You'll have to tell Osmán and Tuca and everyone to let me sleep, tell them not to call me, have them let me sleep."

"Yes," she said, and added, "There's broth."

"Broth, that's it. Have them bring me a cup of broth and I'm going to sleep."

The Art of Cutting Precious Gems

HE SLEPT FOR what remained of the day. She heard him; in the night she sensed him moving in the bedroom, heard him open the door to the bathroom, run the water, return to bed. That was all, and the next day he continued to sleep. Tuca prepared a platter of *gasgos* and waited for him at lunch. But she had breakfasted alone and she dined alone.

"Put them away," she told Tuca, "until this evening."

She could not write that day. The woman in the novel called her, perhaps, or she thought she called her just because she could not answer the call. She busied herself with other things: she worked with Osmán; working ahead, in truth, anticipating the gathering, the baling, the next boat that would come down from the north blowing its whistle twice before the curve, silence, then two more times to announce it was coming, it would tie up, it would wait for cargo. There was something definitive in that getting ahead, like saying, now everything is finished, I'll close up and go. And while she ordered and filed papers before she left, looking over them quickly to see what they were, receipts, invoices, whatever, and the date so they would be in order, she heard another life, but not that of the writing, another, the one she was beginning, I'll close up and I'll go. Nothing could be heard from the bedrooms or, closer, from the empty room that was the center of the house. True, the doors were closed, but even so she could have heard footsteps, sensed, even without hearing, that he was coming toward the office. She thought she was stunned by the whisper of the papers in her hands, the way the typewriter keys sometimes shut out any murmur of the house while Celina spoke, she spoke to her; but it was not so, it was the silence, this time, that covered the sound.

In the silence, in the sometimes dangerous silence, without mazurkas and without the death rattle of the wind that stirs sand into funnels, bends back the branches and angers the waters of the river, she thought, oh, she thought, imagined, contemplated behind closed lids what had been tormenting her, which was the presence—ferocious face of absence—the presence of that man, his return in delirium or in a dream that, because he had not died, had become reality. An image restored, reappeared, now no longer in the drowsiness of a hallucination; it would appear in the opening of that doorway and he would say to her, perhaps—what would he say to her, that she must go? Or no, nothing, and then never again would he address her, not even to ask the reason for the money in the bank and not in the house as he had decreed.

Osmán, she would tell him, boarded the boat each time at a different hour of the afternoon or the morning; there was no danger, she would tell him. Or no. If she had to leave—and then she thought of the boat that carried Osmán to the port, Osmán with the money sewn into the lining of his jacket and she also thought of the worn-out little boat that would carry her far away from there but no, never to the city in the north, and she thought of her clothes hung in the wardrobe and of the *curús* under the rotten bark and the floorboards. Everything, she said to herself, everything one does at the small scale with one's life, that is what decides how it will pass, how it will weave the plot, so brittle, that separates us from others.

"No," she said aloud.

"Ma'am?" asked Osmán from the door to the office.

"Nothing," she said, "I was thinking out loud," and she even smiled.

Osmán said something about the work outside and left, maybe thinking she would follow.

No, this time to herself, no longer out loud and even fearing someone might hear her, no, she would not go. She could not. Not, obviously, to the cold city where she had been born and had lived until Bridget, until what happened to Bridget. No. Nor to the village of the Chetvas because they were not her people even though they said they were. They were not hers nor was she one of them. She was only a *derba-nuru*, a wise woman who looks after other women and whom, depending on the moon, everyone, not just the women, everyone asks for advice. She belonged to no one, untouched, and the sooner she understood that, the better, because then she would not have to be constantly asking herself if she would go or if she would stay, whether the city of the north or the village of the Chetvas, whether dresses and thick stockings and gloves and jackets, or linen suits and tall boots or yellow skirts and bare feet.

Everything, ever since that bloodied face in the newspaper, everything had been taking her and carrying her from one supposed destination to another one, no less illusory. And now, it seemed to her, she heard something in the bedroom beyond the room that was nearly round, something, another of those, some other one of those small things that establish unforeseen links, impossible knots, that which perhaps—with no reason whatsoever —is called fate, sign, shadow, perhaps chance.

Umbra

HE TURNED OVER in bed, thinking the noises he heard from beyond the bedroom walls were bothering him. He did not open his eyes. He turned over again. The noises didn't bother him, not really, they did not bother him. Yet there was something there that, halfway asleep, he was not able to understand. He tried to wake up all the way and find out what was happening around him, but was not able to. He slept again, this time without dreams and without noises.

But at mid-afternoon, he didn't know it was mid-afternoon, he only knew that now he was going to be able to hear the noises and not only hear them but know what it was all about; at mid-afternoon, seated on the edge of the bed, he had the sense that he was at home. He did not say it to himself that way, he did not even say to himself that something different was happening, something was intervening to twist what is sometimes called fate; but he knew it, it was true, he had returned. He went to the bathroom and ran the water. In the bathtub with the warm water that rose slowly over his hips, his waist, his chest, he thought that was it, it was the familiar noises that let him know he was at home. And then it was as if time moved backward and he floated in the maternal waters and could feel himself in a way the victor.

It had not been the *morcós* or the bandits of the interior or the jaguars, but something he had heard spoken of without completely believing it. Renegades, if one had to call them something. Men of different tribes, different kinds, and some women, too, brought together by chance or vengeance around the oases of Membpu, three of them, incredibly fertile and unfortunately close to one another, separated only by the moving dunes that allowed them to watch their prey from above without running any risk at all. They had fallen on them in broad daylight and dragged them to a kind of encampment in which grimy tents made ragged by time and drunkenness and wind and negligence rose alongside others recently stolen, still colorful, wide and comfortable. He learned later that for each tent there had been and evidently would continue to be ferocious battles because it did not matter who stole them, but who conquered them.

Separated from the men, he was the most interesting catch, the only white in the group. They took everything from him, luggage, papers, tools for a week in the desert, even his clothes, looking for what? Not money, money was no use to them, but something, anything that might be useful, from scissors, stockings, lighters, whatever it might be, to sleeping bags and tin cups. And they left him there, naked, lying on the sandy ground in one of the newest tents. Strange consolation, he had thought, this dying in a luxurious tent and not in one of the poorer ones. But the luxurious tents were the most secure: he learned that the same night when he tried to lift an edge, tear the hard and shiny fabric, separate the panels that served as door. Having nothing, not even a pocketknife, a razor blade, it was impossible to escape. For now, he told himself, for now; maybe saying that would help him—what? Die well? Like a hero? Tortured for his intrusion or merely to entertain the barbarians? That night he did not sleep, but at dawn, exhausted, he closed his eyes and drifted into the shadow of his eyelids as if nothing were tormenting him.

He could not, as he had intended, keep count of the days. The half-light in the tent was always the same, night or day. Someone, sometimes a woman, he thought, brought food and water, very little, once a day. And that was all. In the beginning he tried to reject what they brought him, but hunger overcame him and he ate, trying not to identify what he was swallowing. Sometimes his stomach turned and he vomited and the smell of vomit mixed with the smell of excrement and of urine and of sweat. He tried to bury everything in the sand but he hurt his hands and finally contented himself with lying on that yellowish ground, ill, sweaty, and immobile, waiting for that someone to come with another worn wooden dish that would hold another meal that he would try to eat without asking himself questions and that maybe he would be able to keep down and not spend hours trying to hide from himself under the sand.

It seemed to him his body was shrinking and drying out. Sometimes he felt feverish, sometimes he shivered with cold or sweated and the water, the precious water, trickled down from his forehead to his lips where he tried to slurp it up with the tip of his tongue. Outside, always the silence, pierced at times by a cry as unidentifiable as what they brought him to eat. He stopped thinking about escape.

And it was then that in the silence there were no cries but, yes, a scrape, like a scratching or scrubbing, here, close to his head, to the ear that rested on the sandy ground. Maybe it was night. Maybe it was a viper; some animal, one of those that roars with hunger and tears at the flesh with big bites—his flesh. Once again the scraping, the murmur, something, someone, someone who had a voice, not a growl, and with that voice said, let's go! like that, urgent. Yes, it was, it was night.

They walked until dawn, three men and him, two plains- men and one Abu'nakues. One of the plainsmen had reached an understanding with the woman who brought their food, he had asked her for water, more water than she brought, and she had hesitated but at last she brought it. Afterward she began to stay with them longer than necessary and little by little, one by one, like in a game, they began to touch her and to ask her to show them her bottom and her sex and take off what she was wearing and they'd laugh and keep touching her. They took her one at a time while the others looked on and approved, and although they did not vomit up their food, the smell of sweat and of heat and of semen and aching bodies surrendered to other bodies began to fill the tent which was not, as his was, one of the best; on the con- trary, it was full of holes and slits through which filtered sun and nocturnal insects. Two of the men attempted to escape through one of the holes but, said one of the plainsmen, they rushed it. They killed them only a few meters from the tent and the woman did not appear for several days and a boy or what seemed to be a boy but could have been an old man, all skin and bones and nearly blind, his rheumy eyes barely open, brought their food.

They did not know how many days had passed without the woman's return, but she came back at last, this time her forehead adorned with red and white paint and her hair woven in a kind of braid that showed small, almost sparkling stones at every turn.

"What did you do with her?" he wanted to know.

The men gave him to understand that no, they had not killed her; they had deceived her, true, telling her they would take her with them, and thus they had acquired clothing and even boots. Nothing more than that, but enough for the hike. They knew they had to walk toward the northeast but they had neither food nor compass nor anything that would help them save the sun that marked the way—cruelly, it's true. They knew they were going to meet other groups and believed, trusted, that they would be friendly.

They were. At last they rested and ate and drank water, not a lot, what was absolutely necessary so that their flesh would not fall off them in chunks, become ash or bark. At last they knew that perhaps they would return to La Preciada.

The water was getting cold in the tub but he did not want to get out even if it became entirely cold. The dream, that was all well: he had slept all that he needed to and now he wanted to ask himself what it was that had happened in those days of hell. Hell must be something similar, he thought. And he also thought, *I have already been through that, I thought I was going to die but I was not afraid, I was disgusted, my body helped me, my dirty, hungry body, the one that made me hear the silence and in the silence a piano, it helped me to live, I could not renounce air, what was in the tent was not air, there must not be air in hell and I needed air.*

He left the bathroom and dressed, stroking the clothes he put on. The storm, he thought, those storms that one does not forget, those days in the tent, in the desert, with those men with whom one could barely communicate, and now this.

He opened the door and left the bedroom at the same moment she entered the room that was almost round, from being so octagonal, through the door to the parlor.

He asked if it was true that she hated him and she said no and afterward she asked if he was going to throw her out.

"Are you going to throw me out?" she said.

He said: "No."

And she was able to see the hands of that man who was her husband, that man, the one who had returned but not so she might bury his body diminished by the wind, eaten by the jaguars and the sun, but rather for this, only for this, nothing more.

The Tyrant of Athens

AT LAST THE wind—white hand, face of a boy—had stopped blowing. From the south, nonetheless, came the imperfect and timid suggestion of a sandstorm, not water from the west but sand, a thousand points as if of fire that would hammer into objects and animals, causing bellows and sores, until the water rose up in fury and swallowed everything in revenge, or the buttresses of his world bore—without giving in—the weight of the dancing air.

Not fully dark, because the hospitable night holds reflections and does not leave off sealing the outline of the hours, there where the dawn explodes in the east and takes up the cadence of the days. Space, he felt, the infinite, blue space of the crested birds with their curved beaks, spur and caw; space grew around his body like a silent, constant bubble that would not abandon him, not now, strong and elastic as he now felt his flesh in which all things were possible. He spanned the entire world, that of the savannas and the forests, of the great rivers, the dunes and the tundra within his arms, under eyes now half-closed on returning from sleep—why not, if everything was there, within arm's reach, if everything could happen in that beloved and detested land to which he had arrived, in which he had lived, in which he had died not in absence, permanently, but rather the complete opposite, so as to come back to live? He felt her moving at his side, as if searching for his body, he thought, or perhaps not his body, not the caress; a slow brush, silence, the air that finally emerges from the throat converted into word, a single word or many that don't know any other way than to climb over one another; no, perhaps only groping toward a more comfortable position against him, an arm, nothing more than the weary arm on that side crossing his right flank and the hand, who knows, far away and ignored until he should move, exposing himself to contact. A blue-green bubble like the world in which storms and cities, hidden springs and stone staircases, that whole pearly net at sunrise, seas, also seas, and rivers, the water split from the reddish skies, called him and boiled around him without him, he who came from the hell without air, thinking of resisting as she had not resisted, why would one do so? Why if she had run toward him as he returned; why if in the night she had said that, that she knew he had not died because she had seen him again and again, at any hour, attentive or preoccupied, seen him return and return to La Preciada long before she had seen him return over the path of sand?

He recognized how pride, ancient horseman of destiny, brief as the lightning flash, rose in his breast; but he knew it was not the pride of having won a trophy (what did trophies matter to him?) but a different pride: that of having been, it seemed to him, he really believed it, of having been, if only for an instant, capable of accepting, without struggle and without regrets, the existence—although perhaps no, not the existence but the arrival, the birth of another being without whom there would not have been this distancing oneself from the world so as to live moment to moment without crossing the limits of a universe without a bottom, undefined, changing, sensitive to touch and sight, and not for that reason to ignore what is called reality, day after day, lord and master of the land and the things settled on the land. Women, he thought clearly now while he tried to find the hand forgotten beyond his right flank, women must feel that, or something similar, that which goes beyond themselves, when they give birth. And then he turned toward her and embraced her once again, very, very carefully.

She did not feel it, it was not exactly feeling but something more hidden, like the weight of all the gestures in the world, decanted when it passed through her throat in the shadows of what she had known, of what was unknown and what had been renounced: the sun was coming out in England. The storms, all the storms stirred in her belly and Odysseus heard in spite of everything the song of the sirens that pierced the mirrors and was his own song. Perhaps he had thought she cried out and, cradled in the voice, he too had spoken words, calming or burning like his hands, or high syllables ending in silence. The sun of England burst in her veins and occupied the space and the time in her arched waist and in the blood's reverberation. She knew that now everything had found its place and she, lady and mistress, was at her own disposal: the river, the words she wrote about injustices and misunderstandings, the unspeakable secrets, the impossibility of writing, life that revives, death that erases everything, the wind from the west and the daybreak loaded with menace. She knew, finally, how the novel ended for Celina, that woman who waits for death, her eyes lit by a landscape that never existed. She knew that now she could finish writing *Uncertainty*.

Outside, while she once more let herself go, emerge, settle down, roll her body in the city of the clouds, there outside as if it had called her, the wind turned and the storm from the west, the dreaded storm, beat against the sand, against the trees hurt by the squall, and threw itself upon the dark water of the river.

Uncertainty

EVELYNNE HARRINGTON

Vanderbilt University Press
Nashville, Tennessee

When people say that nothing happens in their lives I believe them.
But you must understand that everything happens to an artist; time
is always redeemed and wonders never cease.

MURIEL SPARK

Through the window she could see the upper crowns of the trees on the street and beyond them, the stained wall—smooth, stained; spotted and soft like old evening songs—of the apartment building, that one, that building, that blind, smooth wall, across the avenue.

One night, she saw something on that smooth, stained wall, seemingly so distant, as if it were drawn there; something which perhaps was nothing, something that almost certainly did not exist, had never existed, but she preferred to believe that yes, it had been something, she had seen that thing, because apart from herself, only the window and what she saw through it brought her a bit of the outside from which she no longer expected anything.

She knew she was dying; she knew she was dying and knowing it produced neither anxiety nor sorrow. She didn't even think about it much: the moment had come, so why keep worrying at it and complain and torment herself? She wasn't having pains or difficulty breathing or tremors or anything so folkloric as the final death rattle. Her life was leaving her, that was all, slowly, calmly, little by little. The nurses smiled, the doctors gave her little pats on the hand, the IV falling drop by drop carried all the medications she needed, and on the wall of that building a persistent and magnificent landscape sparkled with the sun's gold. It was night when it shone, as if aware that in shining it lit her face, as if to bring light to her eyes, so she would not be in the dark. By day there was nothing: a wall and nothing more, the mute side wall of an apartment building.

She was going to die, yes, she was going to die. She would close her eyes and she would already be on the other side, that germ of the void from which emanated all fear as well as the desperate search to believe in something and where finally, at this point in life she knew that what she hoped for, wanted, was to encounter nothing, not angels or presences or flames or gardens or offices or another rebirth, nothing. Not even anything that would die with her because, she knew, a person lives not only in a world but with a whole world populated as much by memories and ghosts as by people who think and speak, dance and suffer, generations, equipment, music, doctrines, books, films, operas, conflicts, horrors and portents and hopes all belonging to that time which had fallen to her. It would die with her and another world would begin in which others would die, carrying with them all that had surrounded them and that she would no longer know.

Nor did she regret not knowing it, but she did ask herself, true, how it would be to die in another manner, in the water, for example, drowned, sinking down in order to float again when inevitably everything had come to an end. Maybe because her body spoke to her of floating in the form it had come to have, tame now, barely denting the center of the orthopedic mattress, as if weightless, as if she really were in the water. Not in the muddy water of a soft-bottomed river that flows between sand and wind, but in the green or blue sea, clear and slow, where, they say, all the instants of a life are remembered, speeded-up but precise, as if they were happening at that moment. In the water, where everything began, and for that reason other kinds of death did not appear to her. The water. In the landscape over there across the avenue there didn't seem to be water. A murmuring fountain, that's what was missing; a murmuring fountain, although it's true all fountains are murmuring and not only in romantic novels; a fountain, however it might be, would not be bad in that generous, magnificent golden light. A fountain, a stream to cross, a raging river like those that come from the mountains, or fog that condenses in the crowns of the trees, snow, white snow that melts with the arrival of the time of larvae, of green and of sprouts above the soil.

She had not thought of forms of death other than those, the one she was living and the one of the water of the sea. And goodness, if there aren't a lot of ways to die. But she didn't want an accident or a bullet or a poisoning: only the water. Possibly because of that, because if one drowns, she remembers all of her life in an instant. Why not a whole life, all of it, complete, since she always knew that moments are treacherous, they last for centuries or they last a breath or nothing. She had tried to write that: in one of her first novels, when she was young, immortal and ambitious, there had been a character in a novel—which novel was it? what was the name?—a character who could manipulate time according to whim. Or maybe not, maybe what she had written was that he thought he could do so but he was not able to; not in reality, in the reality of the novel. Making time obedient to him was a crazy idea, or even better, it was a pretext, that's what it was. *En Route*, the novel was called *En Route* and she was very proud of the text and of its title, because the route was in effect a route, the route of the journey that carried the protagonist back to the house in which he had been born, and it was also a metaphor for life as a journey. On that route, the route of the journey, and a little less in that of his life, many things happened to the protagonist, Gustavo Marín; she remembered perfectly well that the character, the one in that novel, was called Gustavo Marín; anyway, on that homeward journey and in the life he remembered as he went, went, went (and it seemed to him that he only traveled and was never going to arrive) many things happened in his life, some of them happy, others indifferent, because his was a life without shocks, without too much pain; a few misfortunes and of those few the saddest was the final tragedy, which nevertheless arrived silently, almost softly, without cries or whimpers, when the road neared its end. She believes, if she thinks about it (she doesn't remember that as clearly), she thinks he did not in fact arrive, he died trying to determine how long the instant had lasted, the three months the return had taken him, died in sight of the house around the curve, and that she had thought of Moses who did not reach the land of milk and honey. It wasn't an especially good novel, she had always known that, but neither was it terribly bad.

"Were you awake, dear?" the nurse said. "I'm sorry to bother you, but I have to take your blood pressure, all right?"

Before writing novels she had written poems. Those really were bad. She had attempted everything, sonnets, free verse, old-fashioned ballads, haikus, rhymes, anything, until she was convinced she wasn't a poet. She would have liked it, though, writing verses, being an almost secret author of measured poems that might speak of the sensitive world, of the way everything stops when the one who writes speaks the appropriate words.

"It's very good, very good." The nurse took the little sleeve off and put the stethoscope around her neck, like a necklace; like a shawl, like something necessary, jewel or yoke, for her to completely be what she was. "Do you need anything, dear? Do you have cool water within reach? Don't move your left arm, all right? Anything at all, call me."

Perhaps poets were more—more what?—more perceptive and more prudent; perhaps for them words were not like bridges over the abyss, to say it in a godawful solemn way, but like signals, sometimes luminous, sometimes dark and hidden, that one must know how to obey upon seeing them far off, or even disobey if there is a danger they will turn against the writer. And she finally got used to the novel, and she even found signals that were probably forbidden to poets and that for her were not luminous but evasive but that gave in before her insistence. Much later, more or less when she had written *The Hostages*, she had discovered that the game was entertaining and that she could deceive the words and make them give in even before they had given her any resistance. She had a lot of fun writing that novel, but even more so the next one, *Snowstorms*, with that first chapter that seems to point toward testimonial and then unexpectedly, like a sharp bolt of lightning, a gyroscope of letters and syllables and intentions, goes definitively toward the absurd. Novels aren't like stories, in which one has to be perfect or nothing; novels are like an adventure, *angusta ad augusta*, although it may be impossible to get there. And she had worked for a long time on the novel about the writer who had lost his daughter and whose pain prevented him writing his own novel, *Hidden Variables*. That novel wasn't finished, and now it wouldn't be. She thought, lying on that white bed among so much white—walls, ceiling, the nurses and the needles and the minutes—that she would have had to add the paragraphs she had written in her notebook to the first part of the novel. And she thought the writer's suicide should have had a more decorous and at the same time more lacerating dramatic turn, because the nameless pain that man felt was the true, would have been the true axis of the novel. In any case, it would have been a short novel, not like *The Hostages* at just over four hundred pages, no; it would be, it would have been something more malleable, more to scale. But now, she said to herself later, surprised by her reflections, why think of those things now?

She had written short stories, too, three books of stories. The best was *Viper's Flesh*, but the others weren't bad. She had written *The Golden Horde*, an ironic title if ever there was one, after Ricardo's death, and *Traps* when she had barely begun to publish. Yes, but she didn't remember it too often, perhaps because it had been her first book of stories, written after the novel about the route, and she wasn't very sure of the results.

She never stopped saying, in interviews or in notes about her books, that all her life, ever since she was a girl, she had been a good reader, an almost omnivorous reader; but writing, and this she preferred not to say, had not been a decision taken as a result of what she had read and thought about. Well, no: it had begun as a hobby, a pastime, nothing important, writing a diary when she was eleven, twelve years old, at that dangerous age when a whole life's luck may be wagered; but of course, the luck of a whole life can be wagered also at five or at twenty-three or at any other age when, suddenly (it seems sudden but it's something that has been brewing, secretly cooking in the steam of desires) a trivial event or words unsaid decide from that point forward the future direction of all agreements, all rulings, even the resolutions that will never be fulfilled.

In those first years of chaos and of hints, she wrote, if not every day, almost every day in a notebook with soft green covers, with blank pages without lines or squares, and she told what she had done, what she had felt, the hours, what she thought, what she wanted to be or to do, everything. She believed it was everything, because it was a long time later that she discovered it is not possible to say or write or encourage or confront everything and that was another moment when she wagered what some call destiny.

But meanwhile she wrote, and it wasn't long before she began to note down, first as a simple list and later with commentaries and reflections, the books she read. Then she wrote down everything, everything she read, from romance novels to schoolbooks, including the stories she read to her brothers at night and what she found in the school library, books she didn't understand, books that bewitched her, books that made her think of distant lands, books that bored her to death but that she read through to the end, while thinking about something else if necessary, because she was convinced that to leave a book, to not read it all the way to the end, would rob her of all the readings she had already gone through, one by one.

And she found herself one day writing a poem and when she finished it she put away the green notebook with the soft covers, which was running out of blank pages, and said she needed another, and then her father proposed:

"In accounting they are getting rid of the old books. I'll bring you one."

It had hard, thick black covers and the spine and the corners were of chestnut-colored leather. The good thing about the cover, what was really exciting, were the cursive letters that proclaimed "Diary" in gold. Inside, on pages so rigid they were almost cardstock, there were horizontal rows in a pale blue and columns of red vertical lines, but although she would have liked to write on blank pages, it didn't matter; on the contrary, it seemed to her that the meticulousness of the lines was useful for writing poems, the words would follow the direction of the blue lines toward where she wanted them to go without the need to force them, and they would stop before reaching the other sign, the vertical one that would mark the border that should not be crossed.

The mother who watched her write and the father who had brought her the notebook, both thought it was for rough drafts of schoolwork and she could have left it on her nightstand and they would not have opened it; they would not even have given it a glance. But the twins who would rummage through all her things and even open the wardrobe in her bedroom and snoop inside, they were a danger. After thinking about hiding it under her nightgowns, behind the shoeboxes, in the cupboard in the scullery hidden by the big platters that were almost never used, she put it where everyone would see it, between the geography book and the math book, and although she had not yet read "The Purloined Letter" or *The Man Who Was Thursday*, she proved that the twins couldn't see it.

In what she remembers of that life, although the sea does not surround her or drown her or rock her or kill her, in that time, she recalls, they lived in the house on Avenida del Puerto which was later called Comodoro Estévez although everyone, always, called it the coast road or the port street. It was a large house, a little sad, with iron balconies on the first and second stories. Upstairs, she had a large bedroom in which fit, along with the bed and the wardrobe, a desk like the ones at school, with its bench and its lid that raised. Her brothers slept downstairs, in a room that gave onto the garden, and her parents close to her, at the end of the corridor. On the ground floor there were, in addition to the boys' room, a dining room, a large living room, her father's study, the kitchen, and the servants' rooms.

On Saturdays her parents went out to eat with Aunt Leila and Uncle Miki, and she was responsible for taking care of the twins: she had to make sure they ate and that they went to bed at ten, since it was Saturday, and not at eight-thirty as on weekdays, and she had to read them a story. The twins didn't like the stories she read them. They said, *Again?* And also *Who cares about that?* and *I'm fed up with riddles, do you hear me? Fed up!* Then one Saturday night, a stormy night to top it all off (although if you think about it, that was why she had chosen it), one night she read them "The Black Cat" and Robi, who was an idiot, who had always been an idiot and would remain one, started to cry. She told him if he kept crying he was going to hear the black cat meow through the wall and the only thing she achieved was that Robi kept crying and hid under the covers while Leo pretended to laugh, but he was plenty scared, too.

That night the two of them told her enough, they were too big now and they didn't want her to read them stupid stories ever again and she answered that she couldn't stand them and it was all over and never again, who did they think they were.

"I won't take care of them anymore," she told her mother the next morning. "I won't take care of them. As far as I'm concerned, they can eat or not eat, they can go to bed or not go to bed, they can sleep or not sleep, what do I care?"

That wasn't the issue. The issue was fear. She's not afraid now, of death or of nothingness, but in those years, she was afraid, and the fear was fear of something, she didn't know what. The fear was more important than any other impression or feeling or whatever it might be because she knew, the objects in the house that spoke to her in code told her every day, she knew that behind a door or inside a wardrobe, there would be, hidden, ferocious, gathering strength so as to appear when she let her guard down and no longer expected it, there would be something without a name, something dark, with eyes, smelling of damp and blood, or worse, a little round pink smiling face that, treacherously, would little by little transform itself into a viscous, soft substance, pure flesh without bones that would jump on top of her, that would prevent her from crying out, asking for help, moving. She knew something would emerge some place, something that would surprise her, would make her heart stop, that heart of hers, that cursed heart, the one that beats dangerously always close to the abyss, always as she learned later but as she already suspected, because she had seen the characters in books shake their heads and move their lips, habitually naked, threatening, seen them emerge from the page and speak to her, tell her what she did not know, what she had believed she would never know, what she did not want to hear, what no one had ever said in this world, under this sky.

She wanted to be like them: worded, afraid. No, she wanted to be the witness, the one who speaks, the one who says, with fear. No, not that either: she wanted to sit down beside each one of them, those who were afraid, touch them, cry with Eleutheria, howl with Iphigenia, die like Embleghorn, flee like Helen, survive like Horace, behead, oh Judith!, the tyrant, dream like the crazy man harping on his single string and bathe in the blood of her enemies while in the night of misery and crimes she takes up the sword because pardon does not arrive. That's what she wanted, and to tremble with fear before the faces of the dead.

It took her nearly twenty years to understand that what she was looking for was the form her stories would have when she told them, but because fear is persistent, she resisted the novels in which some of what pursued her at night would surely be revealed in the lines, and she began writing those poems that had been no use to her—but one of her critics had said, yes, had once said that the exercise of poetry had given her the limpidity of language. Did they say limpidity? Maybe not, maybe something that sounded like that to her, like a thing without color, like insipid broth or frosted glass, or like an Aero chocolate, something like that, wavy, easy to suppress.

While the golden landscape lasts and she looks at it from time to time and asks herself if she will be able to sleep in spite of that sun, a tiny shadow makes her raise her eyes and there on the edge of the other wall, on the panel of lights and graphs marking who knows what, the level of oxygen, the beats of her pulse, the drops of the IV, whatever it might be, up there a small gray spider, barely visible against the white wall, weaves uselessly a web she does not see but that is surely there. What she saw, what caught her attention, was the movement. That, the movement that is not even a shadow, that swayed to her right, up there where it was so easy for her to see. It's because spiders, she knows, move like ballerinas, like the shadows of ballerinas, in silence, softly.

Seven years, she isn't sure, but likely no more than eight, the thread of a spider, the thread Ariadne wove, from the eaves to the deck chair, making a slight curve, the thread of the spider sparkled in the morning and she looked at it and decided God existed. If a thread silvered in the sunlight endures the gaze of a child and without noise, without voice, without scent, without anything, keeps swaying boldly in spite of the rotation of the earth, in spite of the law of gravity, of comets and logarithms, as if ignoring everything or casting it aside, sticky and magnificent, the something she is unaware of and perhaps will never be able to explain holds up the fangs of the dinosaurs, the mortar that keeps the eave in its place, the wind from the west, the shadow of the ballerinas, books, fruits, the hands of the clock, the paint of the pictures, and in addition to all that, herself standing there, looking, her feet in her shoes with straps. It didn't matter to her that Lucifer had made the spider and God the star because the fallen angel was still an angel and it's certain God loved him, very certain, more than certain and precisely because he's God; and so the *Loxosceles reclusa* that she knew as a box spider has a part of the beauty of the stars and in the stars live those little balls with eight legs that run to find safety in the cracks of tree trunks.

"Might one ask what you're doing, standing there like a fool? Come on, let's go, hurry, I need the flour."

So it was a Sunday, because her mother needed the flour. The thread sparkled against the shadow of the trees and thanks to the strand of silver and light, she glimpsed the order of the universe. She didn't dare even to breathe—flour, her mother needed flour—much less to leave that place, but then it occurred to her that if she moved, breathed, blinked, all of that would also enter into the order of the universe, it would find its place, and although she might not see the silver thread in the sunlight, she would always know that God exists like the squares on a board meant for an incomprehensible game, and for that reason she was going to be able to take her first communion without guilt or apprehension, but she also knew she was not going to say anything to Señorita Amelia or to the other girls.

The little gray spider rested a moment and she asked herself if it needed that rest in order to manufacture at the base of the palpus that solid yet tender substance, silvery, without taste or scent, stubborn, that would be stretched into other threads so as to connect the eaves with the deck chairs, the leaves of the trees with the door hinges, the blinds, the chimneys, the pointed world that comes out of the earth. Afterward it began again, the almost invisible little spider, and it worked hard, it came, went, circled, trotted, squandered threads that she couldn't see as if it were saying to her, *look at me, don't look too much over there because the landscape is going to be erased under that gaze of yours that goes back again and again, greedy for light.*

She didn't want to think the golden landscape could be worn out under her gaze, disappear, not return the following night. Neither did she want to think the little gray ball that spun around up there knew something about the luminescent landscape that she did not know. She was afraid it might, because she had guessed back when she was very young that spiders are small, wise beings, velvety, inoffensive and fearful; the gray spiders in the corners of the ceilings, the predators, the *Mygale*, all of them, and if she was able to get one of them to walk over her neck or her arms, she would feel a delicious shudder, something like the understanding of what moves all the secret little animals, those that hide from people's claws.

She had never written about that, just as she had never written her memoirs. She had not written about her parents or her brothers or the houses she had lived in or the schools she had gone to or what the dances were or what was talked about, what was said when she was fifteen, or about her illnesses and her family and her friends and her trips and especially about the task of writing. She had not written about Ricardo's death or the room so octagonal it was almost round, nor the bitterness nor the revolver, the threat, the loneliness, the late music of small pleasures.

It is also true that she had written about all of that, only without naming it. She ran and cried and loved and was born and shouted with her characters and that was her own and her true happiness: that which she had been able to find in life. Strange, or not so much, that now when she was dying she should keep thinking about her life, that she should tell it to herself. It was comforting, as if in speaking it, she relived everything that had overwhelmed her in those moments that return with the high tide in an unexpected turmoil.

The nurse would come and put the thermometer under her arm, *dear, don't move, keep it there*, and when she left she would stop looking toward the side with the gray spider and she was going to immerse herself in the landscape she saw during the nights. No one would ever see it, she alone, and she would not tell anyone about it, ever. She almost smiled thinking of the face Ricardo would have made if she had seen the landscape then, when they lived together, and if she had told him about it. She had come to know him so well that she could anticipate his smallest gestures, those that would have been almost imperceptible to the world at large and even to he himself. He would have looked at her with that *ay*-Celina-the-things-you-think-of face and would have shook his head slowly so as to smile afterward and say good, she could use that in her next novel. She came to believe that what she saw when he looked at her was premonitory. Nonsense, she told herself, she remembers that, but she had also said in a lecture or a roundtable or a preface or something similar that those who write live on nonsense, and it had been the absolute truth at that moment and perhaps it was now, as well.

His last expression, for example. She knew it was the last. Did she really know? She knew? She feared? She could never be sure. Perhaps not, she had not known. But sometimes she thought she had, that life with him had given her that clarity, which had allowed her to see what was to come. And other times she was reasonable and sensible again and she knew that no, to guess once everything had ended was almost like the smug expression of a cheap magician showing off the mirror trick, an easy and hollow display. A scam.

When everything was over and they left her in peace so she could go back over the pain and the surprise, in those moments she told herself no, it had not been that, she had not known, had not had a presentiment, that she had, held, perhaps nurtured a secret desire that he should not return; not that he should die, but that he should not return. She told herself *don't wait for me, I don't know when I'll be back* had been no more than that, *don't wait for me, I don't know when I'll be back*, not a farewell. Because, and this was something she seemed to know without any hesitation, because he had not wanted to die; not to return, who knows, maybe yes, yes, but not to see how one, ten, thirty seconds, seconds like centuries, how many seconds later the plane is going to shatter down there below and he and all the rest are going to die crushed, broken, limbs scattered over the countryside, was the plane at that moment flying over the countryside? No, it wasn't in the country. It had been in the sea, the sea, to die as she had dreamed by drowning in the green water, taut and blue. Was the sea as hard as the earth and so it was all the same if the machine fell from up there onto the countryside, into the sea, onto the ice, the salt pan, or anywhere else?

She had met him at her home, her parents' home. She was twenty-six and the twins were eighteen; she worked as an accounting clerk in a bank and her parents, especially her mother, would have liked for her to marry. It didn't seem entirely right to them that she should write and go around with artists and writers who everyone knows are a little shady, always looking for new sensations to give them inspiration—right?—never mind the fact that a poet, a novelist, doesn't earn much, not enough to support a family and they didn't want their daughter to be the one who supported her husband, that just wasn't done. Not among decent people, at least.

Mariano wouldn't be, she knew, all that her parents might have wished, but he came pretty close.

"If you want to stay," she told him, "I think my mother made almond cake."

"I can't," Mariano complained. "It's Aunt Virginia's birthday and we're all going. What if, instead of me staying, you and I went to the party together?"

"Oh, no," she said, laughing.

"We'll see each other tomorrow."

So they said goodbye at the door and she went in and there was Ricardo talking to her father. She didn't know his name was Ricardo and if she had known, so what. It was nothing to do with her: she gave her father a kiss, greeted the man who was talking to her father and went to the kitchen to see her mother.

Ricardo's father had died when he was nine years old and his sister six. They were raised by their mother and grand-mother, two women who more than mother and daughter seemed like sisters. Tall, thin, dry, white, gray haired, they did not lack for gestures of affection toward the children. They were determined to do everything possible so that they might be happy. And as far as one can be happy in childhood, he and Elvira were.

Very Catholic, they taught them to pray, to go to Mass, to confess and take communion, respect the days of obligation, learn catechism and sacred history, make promises to the Lord and give flowers to the Virgin, obey the commandments and guard the purity of their bodies and their souls. At age twenty-three, Elvira had entered into religious life in the convent of the Catalinas. Ricardo never knew if his mother and grand-mother had felt happy or at least proud of his sister's deci-sion. True, oddly or perhaps not so odd, his sister's decision to become a nun caused him to abandon religion and its duties. The two older women made a few attempts to return him to the fold, but they gave up in defeat when they saw there was no point: Ricardo had become a staunch enemy of religion, not just of the church, but of any religion. Fanatics, he said. They had stolen his sister, they had surrounded him with an enormous absence, and, worse, with an empty, quiet past that he was not able to reawaken with memories or with the spell of her voice or with sorrow. Thunder and lightning no longer mattered to him and he never again climbed a tree waiting for the held breath or the wide-open eyes fixed on him from down below. Or maybe all of the affection of a lonely boy that he felt for her was nothing more than an excuse, and his abandonment of the faith had been developing little by little from the time he was an adolescent until the morning on which he saw her dressed as a novice, so happy, as she seemed.

All of that had happened years ago. When she met him, when she saw him for the first time at her parents' house, Ricardo was selling insurance to pay for his law studies. They married a year after seeing each other for the first time at Celina's parents' house, and much as he insisted, writing letters even to the bishop, Elvira did not receive permission to attend the wedding. They buried his grandmother two years later and his mother not long after, at the time she published *White Sea*, which had been an unexpected success. By then her mother had died, Leo lived in Brazil married to a woman from Bahia, he had four children and made jewelry with semiprecious stones, and Robi was a bachelor, he lived with their father and worked at whatever he could find without ever lasting too long or too short a time in any one place. Robi liked just one thing, two things: collecting stamps with pictures of automobiles on them and dancing the tango.

They did not have children, they neither made much effort to have them nor suffered sadness or frustration when they did not. She was earning prestige and sometimes money with her books, especially when they were translated into other languages. And Ricardo, in partnership with two colleagues, took care of the practice and seemed satisfied with his life.

"Did you call, dear?"

"No," she said.

"Ah, I thought, let's see, no, the bell isn't on. But you weren't sleeping, were you?"

"No, but I'm fine."

"We're going to give you a little pill. The doctor said you have to rest."

"But I am resting," Celina said. "I don't need sleeping pills."

"Come, come, we have to listen to the doctor, you know that. They're tiny, see? With a little swallow of water, they go right down. That's it, very good, you'll see how the rest does you good."

"Hmmm," she went, without opening her mouth.

"See you laaa-ter," the nurse sang.

She's a good woman, she thought, *and she spends her night taking care of sick people and she even seems contented, I almost feel bad having to trick her.* She spit the pill into her hand and threw it, without moving her left arm, up in the direction of the little gray spider. She knew it would land on the lighted console that marked her pulse or her cardiac rhythm or whatever it might be. Click, a tiny, tiny sound, and so it was. The little spider didn't bat an eyelid.

If she had time remaining (she knows she does not) she would write a story with spiders; not like Kipling's, with real spiders, spiders that move in a shadowy spider garden that never or very seldom sees the sun. The ground only warms up during a couple of very early hours in high summer, when the rays are not so strong and there isn't much time either, when that sun would not reach to burn even the tips of the blades of grass. The spiders, velvety, succulent and timid, would feel happy in that garden; no one would show up to bother them and they would stretch their threads in every possible direction and a gentle wind would come and destroy them so they could stretch them once again. It would not be a fable with bugs that speak nor with a moral: it would be a story with conflicts and adventures appropriate to spiders; and in spite of the threats, the people who one day invade the garden ready to chop down the trees and let the sun come in, the storms, the cats that extend their claws and swat, the unexpected snow, all would be straightened out at the end and it would return to being exactly the same as it had been at the beginning, at the beginning of the story when they danced, happy and carefree, playing at being ballerinas' shadows, weaving shimmering threads like songs, like celestial messages, murmuring voices of murmuring fountains.

Perhaps she could write it. Perhaps if she asked the nurse for a ballpoint and a notebook, she could write it without moving her left arm, *raise the back of the bed for me, bring the rolling table closer, another pillow, please, that's it, no, no, I don't need anything else, a little silence, tell the doctor on call not to come, everything is fine.*

She couldn't; she knew she couldn't. For as much as her body was comfortable against the pillows, it would be impossible now to write a story. Nonetheless, she recognized the longing to write, which she thought she had left behind when she learned the diagnosis and the little time she had left. The longing that would never leave her in peace. That *never* was now meager and fragile, but it would be, as it had always been, present and demanding, invincible. It had appeared with the black notebook with leather corners that said "Diary" in cursive letters on the cover and it had been with her always and when she went against it, it turned around restlessly, it attacked her pitilessly and made her suffer a kind of intimate madness, internal, secret, that no one noticed. But when she obeyed that longing, well, then it was—what was it? She no longer asked herself that question because now she knew the answer.

At one time she had called it happiness and now she knew, she knew as she had always known, understanding it without thinking about it, that it was much less and much more; she knew, because she had seen it, that it was being able to go into the golden landscape of sun that appeared every night far off on the wall, smooth and stained by day, made arrogant with light by night. She would no longer have time now, but she almost didn't care because she had once again felt the longing to write a story and had rediscovered what happiness was.

She could remember—more than remember, relive—the effort (because when she had begun to write it was an effort) that she made in order to achieve the instant of herself in which everything flows and happens without her slowing it down; the instant in which one is convinced it is possible to choose what she is going to write, the short instant in which she almost sees or hears the text that does not yet exist. And later, when she had acquired that flexibility of spirit that only comes of working day in and day out, one hour and every hour (because that, the longing to write, never stops) later the ease, like a children's song, a jabberwocky, inexplicable to everyone but her, with which anywhere at any time of day or night, she let herself be assaulted by words, even knowing many of them would be lost forever. It didn't matter, because all of them belonged to her and she would find others; she wouldn't even find them: she had only to let them come, dress them as one might dress a child in the warm hollow in which they lined up around her, words, what she lived for, had lived. She had been permeable to everything she heard and saw and read. She had let the world enter her not only through her eyes but also through the eight feet on the ground, through the white belly, through the chelicerae that distill the poison's liquor, through that heart still present in the lights on the console, through the steps in the sun. Words also, to distill poisons as well.

Did others see what she saw? Did anyone hear that voice that doesn't resonate in the ears or in the blood or in the throat but in the invisible wall, the hard air of everything that has been said, everything that has been written in the world? Who? Maybe Robi, who had no common sense. Maybe women who, like her, are going to die tomorrow. Maybe madmen or the mentally deficient or Juana on horseback or the executioners' poet, or the woman from Magdala, but not the night nurse—although, why not? She didn't know, she deceived her but she did not know, she could not know what the night nurse was like.

No. Not at any rate those who lower their eyelids when the light bothers them and accept the world's titles with pleasure. Not those who have never wanted to investigate the path of the air, invent their lives starting with a lament that like a leaf of gold becomes stuck in the trachea. But she was not unique or exceptional. She had intended, and that was all, to trace the furrow opened in the damp black soil, fragrant with charcoal and hail, that and none other, opened by the multitude that had passed that way before her and had left it to her eyes, her feet, tempting, disproportionate, resonant. She didn't feel it was an achievement, much less a great feat. She had lived that way because she had wanted to live that way, dedicated to applying words to everything that was not as it should have been and never—and of that she could be proud—never had she felt sorry for or envied the sad or dry or silent souls. They had awakened her smiles now and again, or a few tears, like Myrtha.

Her cousin Myrtha with a y after the m and an h after the t, who was the daughter not of Leila and Miki but of Susana, her mother's younger sister, and Lionel, an airhead according to her father and a mixed-up boy according to her mother, Myrtha with y after the m et cetera used words as if they were old rags, just like that, without any care, never mind love or even inclination. To Myrtha words were useful for complaints and demands; when she needed to say what she felt, she could not: little cries came out in *eeee* and *oooo* and giggles. And shrieks of terror if she happened to see a spider. Ridiculous girl that she had laughed at, ridiculous girl with ringlets who she had indeed hated until she felt the hate was drowning her, and she smiles when she remembers it was precisely because Myrtha with a y and so forth had blond ringlets and a round face and two brothers like her but no twins and also a sister named Elysabeth also with a y after the l and an h after the t; that was what made her unbearable, she was so blond and so hesitant that she was overwhelming: there were years in which Myrtha with a y occupied an enormous space in her life and she, Celina, did not know how to take away from her that territory of delicate voice, dimples, little embroidered dresses and that Bécquer recitation, *in the dark corner, perhaps forgotten by its mistress.* She sometimes thought Myrtha was a caricature and other times asked herself if she too wouldn't be happy in that other life that brushed against her own.

They get along so well because they grew up together, her mother and Susana said together in unison, but it wasn't true. Myrtha looked at her sideways or, when there was no other choice but to look at her straight on, made a face as if she were looking at something very disagreeable. Celina took her to her bedroom, she went to her bookcases, and she said, "Have you read *Ariel?* Oh, no? And *The Glass Bead Game?* Not *Jean-Christophe* either? Sweetheart, what have you read, if one might ask?"

The other girl seethed and invented boyfriends, Celina was sure it was all pure fantasy, except once it was true and Myrtha stayed with Fredy who had a cleft chin and brows like Mephistopheles and a nose like a Greek god, and then the one who seethed and also cried a little was Celina. *You'll pay me back*, she thought again and again during the month, more or less, until André Gide and Aldous Huxley and Somerset Maugham fell into her hands and she stopped caring about Fredy and Myrtha and Mephistopheles and even the Greek gods. *They get along so well*, Susana said, and she laughed and said, "Isn't it so?"

And afterward Myrtha had gotten married and gone to live in the United States, to Miami, of course, where she stayed so long Celina forgot about her and only remembered her existence when Susana showed up crying that *her* Myrtha had gotten divorced and was coming back to the country.

"Within a month. Oh, Celina, you have gotten along so well with her, you're going to be very kind when you see her, right? I mean, to help her get through this bad time."

She said yes, of course.

How silly to remember Myrtha, on this night that must be about to end, so, so brief. Maybe it was late, maybe the darkness was slipping through her fingers. Maybe it would dawn soon and the landscape on the wall would fade away and she would have to wait for another night in order to see it again. Maybe Nelsi would come, the nurse with the little pill, and change her IV bottle. Maybe at midmorning she would have visitors.

Or no? Or might she still have two hours of quiet darkness?

From the other side of the world, or perhaps not so far as the other side of the world but very far, very far to the east crossing a continent and an ocean, a man whom she would no longer recognize even if she saw him up close, next to her bed for example or sitting in a chair that Nelsi would bring or standing at the window, a strong, heavyset, and carefree guy had just gone to bed after a very satisfactory day. Naked on the bed, hands crossed behind his neck, watching the ceiling fan turning its blades up there almost lazily, he thinks of the new house, smiling faintly and a little bit sorry, not very, admittedly, but a little bit sorry for Saverio who sold it for less than it was worth, poor Saverio who was going back to Europe, richer than when he had left his country, it's true, who was leaving but who didn't want to go to what his wife and daughters called civilization so the girls could study in good schools and marry good catches who would take them on honeymoon to Greece and make them blond children who would speak English without an accent.

He knew even before closing the deal that he would have to make a few repairs: he doesn't need four bedrooms, so he will take down one of the walls and get himself a master bedroom that is nice and big, with two windows to the south that will give him sun in the winter and shade in the summer and two more bedrooms, one that will be used as an office and the other a spare that for the moment he will furnish with armchairs, bookcases, and a floor lamp. Perhaps in the future, he could have a piano in there, always assuming he could acquire a piano in good condition on the island or, if not, have one brought from the mainland. An upright piano, nothing special, to try to remember the songs of his childhood. *He has good fingers*, Grandmother Artemia said when he was still unable to reach the pedals.

The veranda is fine. With just a touch-up, it will look like new. The kitchen: he would have to modernize the kitchen, enlarge it, put what they now call an island in the center and make more shelves and buy a new refrigerator, install an exhaust fan. The master bath is fine, the other is all right and the downstairs powder room is fine, too. The floors, well, he'll think about the floors tomorrow, now it's late to be planning solutions.

It's a fine thing, this having a new house; it gives one the impression of starting another life. The man knows what it is to start another life, although if he says aloud or thinks to himself *another life*, he thinks of the earlier one, not this one he is living now, nor the one he's sure he is going to begin when, the house finished and to his liking, he walks through the rooms and looks out the windows and sits down on the gallery with Náyade and, watching the sun sinking, he runs his tongue over his lips to feel the salt the air brings from the sea. No, what he thinks about is the one he left behind, that one he still doesn't know if he fully remembers.

He came out of the lavatory trying to make out row nineteen at a distance, looking for the round yellow head of the boy who was beside him reading a newspaper in English, when he felt the blow. It was as if they had jolted him with a weapon so powerful it took in his whole body: all of him felt the violent shake that came with the noise of a crack opening in the earth, only he wasn't on the ground and his feet in white slippers with the name of the company in blue rested on a sky blue and gray carpet that covered the entire aisle. He also heard a voice that shouted at him, shouted something at him, it shouted *return to your seat!*, but he wanted to return to his seat in row nineteen, and he heard cries that were directed not to him but to no one, just cries.

He swayed for a moment, heard a crunch of china glass metal breaking and that was the last he knew. He knew, some minutes or some hours or centuries later, that he had to keep himself afloat.

The sea was warm, he had no shoes or coat and he could swim. He thought he had swum, knowing he could not get far. At some point he saw something like a shadow on the horizon and he thought he was going toward some place but no, they were clouds, a few frayed dark clouds that gradually lifted until they left the sky looking empty and sterile as always. He kept swimming. Hours and hours passed and the sun and the nights and eternity arrived and he kept swimming.

He felt something, something that wasn't water under his hands and he tried to shake off whatever was disturbing his swimming.

"Relax," someone said, "don't uncover yourself, if the sheet bothers you we can fold it."

The doctor was English but he also spoke French, Italian, and Spanish. His Spanish wasn't the best in terms of pronunciation but he used the verbs well and he had an acceptable vocabulary.

"What is your name?"

He thought it was an absolutely stupid question and didn't answer.

"Do you remember what happened to you?"

"No."

"Were you aboard a boat?"

"I don't know."

"A yacht, a fishing boat, a lifeboat?"

"I don't know."

Monosyllables, it's true, but even monosyllables tired him.

A week passed and they sat him in an armchair beside the window. Two days later he could go out to the gallery helped by a nurse. A month passed and now he moved almost comfortably. He waited for the doctor to arrive.

"When will Doctor Maurois come?" he asked.

And when at last he arrived and saw the patients and gave instructions to the nurses, then he left the wards and approached him with a gesture of greeting and he knew it was the moment to prepare himself for at least two hours, sometimes more, of conversation. It was the part of the day that justified the others, hours of weariness and boredom and sometimes even a muffled rancor that he tried, almost always with success, to distance from himself.

They talked a little of this, a little of that, he trying to remember, Maurois trying to suggest something that might awaken his memory. He made jokes about his last name, that an English doctor should have the name of a French writer, come on.

"My mother was English," the doctor said, "my father French but he lived in London and I was born there."

He thought for a while.

"You know about writers, that's certain. Could it be you're a writer?"

He laughed.

"Journalist?" Maurois insisted. "Critic, professor?"

But they didn't get anywhere.

He ended up thinking it was true what they imagined on the island: they'd been shipwrecked, boat, yacht, something on which he'd been a passenger or a sailor, and he had swum, at first out of pure will and later by pure instinct, until he lost his breath and his memory of what had happened and, what is worse, of all his previous life, and he was picked up by the boat belonging to Miguel Toro, the one-eyed fisherman who caught herring and red mullet and, when he was lucky, a blond fish too. He set himself to think of boats, rafts, enormous transatlantic ships, sampans, sailboats, in case the image that emerged behind the eyes he half closed so as to better see what appeared brought him the memory of something or of someone. And he finally resigned himself.

"What can I do?" he asked Maurois.

"The first thing," the doctor said, "is to go to the police."

So it was that he acquired a name and identity papers with that name they had invented between the three of them: an Englishman with a sense of humor, himself, and a generous islander more interested in cards and women that in shipwreck survivors.

He worked in the hospital for a time, with the maintenance men, all skilled and smiling islanders not too inclined to wear themselves out repairing electrical equipment or broken pipes or cracked floor tiles or vents damaged by the salt.

He didn't want to spend his life at that: he didn't like the hospital, he didn't like the smell of disinfectant, of sickness and death. He wanted to work at something calmer, seated at a desk beside a window at his left through which light came in, writing letters, for example, or inventories or receipts. He went looking for something like that and after trying offices and shops and drying sheds, presses and tinsmiths, he began as secretary and with time was more or less partner of Daniel Stelbaian, a fat Armenian importer of cloth, leather, and wines. The old man died of apoplexy a year later and he, who was now legally named Johnny Keats, was left with the business and, with the profits, he paid the widow the monthly sum they had agreed upon. With a word and a handshake.

He said, "Ma'am, we should sign a contract."

She, who was not a faded Armenian but an impressive dark brunette who wore necklaces of artificial pears, a signet ring, and an ornamental comb in the chignon of her graying hair, told him there was no need.

He thought about the matter of the contract for many days and concluded that he had signed contracts at one time, but he didn't know what about or why or where. Strangely, it wasn't because of the contracts that he began to remember, but rather just because; at least, he believed it was just because, although after much mulling it over he thought maybe it was because of André Maurois and John Keats.

It went well for him. He discovered that he knew how to persuade people, and especially when among those people were distrustful hoteliers and suspicious bar owners and cattle dealers much more distrustful and suspicious than the others. He expanded the business, established an appearance of order with a counter, a scale, a desk, and a strongbox. He built two rooms and a bath above and from Madame Corinne's *pension* he moved to the recently debuted upper floor which he reached by climbing a wooden ladder that he pulled out of the back room that was also a warehouse. Not long after he bought the house on Buaukké hill in which he had lived until now. Soon, as soon as he finished the modifications that the new house was crying out for, he would move to the one that had belonged to Saverio and his family.

By then he knew everything or almost everything and had decided to say nothing to anyone and not to return. It wasn't that he had been unhappy, on the contrary. His mother and his grandmother and Elvira, above all Elvira, had been part of a life he could remember with affection, with a mild, almost agreeable, tepid sorrow that sweetened his mouth and made him turn his head like someone who tries to hear something that is no longer there. Nor had he been unhappy with Celina, but he had become bored, tired of so much literature, so much art, so many books and so many lectures. The first years had been full of projects and discoveries and the need to be together. She had been interested in what he told her and he read what she was writing and everything seemed wonderful and the two felt they had done what they most wanted in life. That lasted a long time, and it faded very slowly, without pain, like a silent nightfall.

Celina wasn't Mrs. Albert Forrester, luckily, but she was surrounded by an invisible wall he could not cross, words that meant one thing to her and the opposite to him, gatherings of writers where he felt like an extra, although, he conceded, maybe it wasn't exactly like that, times when he wanted to rest or go see a shoot-'em-up and she needed to write or to discuss what she was writing. That, sometimes, made him unhappy, but it passed right away. Did she feel the same about him? She seemed contented and she had never brought up a single problem, the kind women bring out on display when what they want is for the husband to leave them in peace and get out of the house. He had a few adventures, with Myrtha, for example, who had lived for years in the United States and, on coming home, already divorced, had practically thrown herself on him and what can a guy do with a woman like her, attractive, silly, and not very pleasant but pretending at the edge of forty-five that she would never again believe in men after her, oh!, dreadful divorce, and desperate to show—and show herself—that she was still desirable? Also with a secretary whose name he didn't even remember, with Pablo Soler's wife, and maybe with someone else, like that, in passing, as if to get some air before submerging again.

And Celina? Had Celina been unfaithful? He could guarantee she had not. It's true one never knows, but Celina was so calm, so solid, she had such a serene temperament, always so much the same, so transparent that one could almost see in her eyes and in her gestures and in her tone of voice what she thought and what she felt. Hers had been a life without tempests and without torments, in which what was most important was writing, and in which all of the happiness and all the surprises came from there, from writing novels.

The more he remembered, the more fixed his decision not to return. Now he was a different man, he was Johnny Keats, the importer, the owner of the big house that had belonged to Saverio Denoël on the main street, a block from the church. Go back to what? To the courts, the hearings, the proceedings, the chicanery, the judges and the prosecutors? It seemed to him all that he had left behind was sterile, dry, brittle; that in contrast on the island everything has meat, juice, color, heft; that everything is succulent, the women, the earth, the trees, friendship, the sea and the shore; that everything smells of a tumultuous and musical life.

That life may also smell of rot, of rancor, of squalor, of garbage and betrayal, and in fact they had not hidden from him stenches or plagues; and he could almost tell himself that he had looked for a few of them, impelled by naiveté or malice; but it was preferable to pull back from the privations and the dangers, rather than become bored beyond endurance among phrases that no longer mean anything, faces that always have the same studied, smug expression, neat ties on top of well-ironed shirts, sounds and voices that announce neither happiness nor misfortune, tasks when it's clear from the start where they'll end up, how and with what bitter taste.

Island, islet, that anomaly of the sea, seemingly isolated and without recourse, rocked by the oldest voice anyone has ever known, that was what he had been wanting. Or perhaps, which is the same thing in the end, not knowing he wanted it, he had ended up finding it and had turned it into longings now past. He had pursued desire or whatever it might be— all that he had in this present life—by winding paths and he could, when someone spoke to him of insularity with that ambiguous tone that goes from the trap of self-pity to the narrow vigilance glimpsed in the eyes of the other, make gestures of agreement. He no longer explained, he no longer contradicted, he no longer demonstrated anything, not to others nor to himself. The discovery was almost dangerous. No, he never thought about the plane, the accident, the efforts the sea had made to swallow him. He thought, it's true, that he had been fortunate. He thought he had forgotten, that softly, without trying too hard, he had learned to remember; and as a result of the memory he thought, he knew, that from then on all of his days were once again forgotten, but this time it was a mild forgetting of objects and gestures and habits.

The house waited for him. On each visit, he imbued it with himself. Empty, without the furniture or rugs or drapes the Denoël women had insisted on bringing from Europe, it seemed more compact, easier to fit into the days that were to come. He went through it again and again, and again and again on other days. He squatted down on his heels and examined the baseboards to look for damp in the foundation. He knocked on the walls trying to determine what there was behind the plaster. He discovered a greenish-gray stain, sticky to the touch, in the anteroom the bedrooms opened onto: there might be a break in a rain gutter. He studied the floors, went through the galleries, ran the water in the baths and in the kitchen; he took possession of every corner and every molding.

It was his house now and that meant he would not return. It meant that on the island and the hill and in the ditches he found a life he could just glimpse and that, he knew, had nothing to do with the names given to those things in the world, that other place, that otherness over on that side of the ocean. He would not climb aboard a boat to return. He would not return. His associates would say, *how awful, poor Ricardo dying like that*, Celina would continue to be happy with her books and her intellectual friends, she would collect his pension and would surely earn more money than she was earning when he had boarded that plane that was now not even a memory, so, so long ago. Why worry himself? In his imitation memory he would return to that other life once in a while and the memory would bring a smile, less enthusiastic than the one caused by the planned improvements he had begun in Saverio's house, in his house.

He never again boarded a plane.

Celina liked to travel by plane. It annoyed her to have to go somewhere by train or in a car or a bus. If the journey was long a plane was inevitable and she was delighted. If it was short and she could choose, she chose the plane, and if she could not, she resigned herself to whatever might come. That was years ago, but for a long time now she had said no to trips when she could not go by plane. *Strange*, Robi said, but she already knew—everyone knew, and everyone, she included, shook their heads as if in resignation, adding a little bit of affection, protection of the weak—that Robi was an idiot, something that had not improved with age. *Strange because when all's said and done*, he said, *your husband died in an aviation accident so you must be afraid, right?* She said no, she wasn't afraid to fly, and it was true. It was also true that she had tried not to remember the day she had learned the plane in which Ricardo was traveling had fallen into the sea and there had been no survivors.

It had been a cold day, too harsh for the time of year, and she had gotten up earlier than usual. She liked to write in the morning, before breakfast, two or three hours until she began to want to drink a cup of coffee, to toast the bread and take the butter out of the refrigerator. But Leo was staying at her house and would surely want to shower and have tea with milk before going to the hospital to visit their father.

He had been in her house for a few days, because she had written to him; she wanted to write to him and not call him on the telephone. She preferred to tell him by letter *Papá is not well, he gave us a fright, it began with dizziness and then signs of absence and blindness that passed quickly. That was the day before yesterday. Robi called me and Doctor Segura told us that in all probability it was a cerebral infarction. He has been admitted to Lister Hospital. He is in no imminent danger, that's what the doctors say, but I would like it, we would like it, if you would come. He doesn't feel well, he complains a lot, he forgets things, he doesn't know where he is.*

It wasn't serious, she told him, but it could become so. It's a goodbye, thought Celina.

From the kitchen she heard the radio Leo had turned on while he shaved. She put water on to boil to make tea. Upstairs, Leo turned off the radio and she saw him come down, slowly, very serious, pale.

She could see again her brother's face, she could see Leo moving very slowly, looking at her, coming closer, so early:

"I would rather tell you myself, rather than you see it in the papers or on television, the news is everywhere, I just heard it on the seven o'clock report, you have to be strong, Celina."

One hundred seventy-six dead in the sea, where they would never be able to retrieve the bodies. So much time had passed when she began to think about a novel she would write that would be called *Hidden Variables* that when she considered the profound unhappiness of Bruno Seguer, she herself had felt no pain. She decided to superimpose them, the knowing she would not even have Ricardo's body, that cold sorrow she felt as a weight below the sternum; to use it for the monologue of Bruno who knows he will never retrieve his daughter's body and who nevertheless looks for it in the middle of his pain, in the vast, ubiquitous and indelible pain of the world that surrounds him, in the faces of women, in the content of words written to be read and reread without stopping. The situations were so different, she told herself, she had not lost anyone in the cellars of horror and shame, and it was then that she finally concluded that no, in the case of her character, in the case of that Bruno Seguer who struggles between a city in the clouds and a pit from which emerge the foul-smelling memories that claim him, the reflection of that sorrow would have to come from somewhere else.

When such things happened to her, she wondered if she wasn't heartless. To use the last torment she herself had felt in her own flesh, the sorrow—but a different unhappiness—she had contemplated in others, the memory of her pain which refused to die and slipped into her days and the spectacle of the pain of others who would feel—what? longing for the presence of someone who should have been there so as to be able to die?—in order to search for, to find a way to say it, or worse, only to remain for a cold instant in suspense, intrigued, thinking how she might put that into words. It's that every day, every instant brings marvel or horror and very often marvel and horror in a single knot to be untied with letters, behind the letters, in the spaces left by what is being said.

Not only in the letters. The music of a piano heard from far away, the song sung off key by a woman hanging laundry on the terrace, the voice, a voice half-heard on passing close to a door on the street. Wonder and panic in a figure is seen in a mirror that is seen in a painting. Marble, excellence, the unwanted decadence of the beauty of the goddesses, the dirge, dirty walls that once hid a rose garden.

Life resembles that, the multiple, Janus laughing, the Victory of Samothrace that may be a flight toward triumph or a descent into hell; that winged and broken figure that from the prow of an unlikely pedestal cries the name of whoever looks at it, the germ of cruelty, of unhappiness, growing in the lap of fortune. When she saw it for the first time, she felt she needed a word that did not exist; that she was at that moment witness to heaven and hell, a privileged visitor able to step onto the marble and open the tombs of all those who had died a death as cruel as it was useless. What use is death, she asked herself. For this, she writes for this, to find out the origin of lights, the destiny of shadows; to feel what her characters felt, Bruno Seguer, Gustavo Marín, Leonor, Suny the one from Malmö, Esther in *White Sea*, Rogelio and Jorge in *Viper's Flesh*, but not to feel it within herself but outside, separated from her body and her soul by the recollection, to see it coming from those around her, from herself, and be able to stop it and slide it toward the way to write it, letter by letter, feature by feature, silence by silence. Up above, the statue of Victory that has no eyes looks at her from the stone and she looks at the statue and tells herself it is as strong as the thread of a spider hung from the eaves in the sun, sparkling sticky and curved in the solitude of all that has been created, all that is going to die.

She had felt betrayed, stunned and empty, on learning that Ricardo had died, that he would never return, she would never hear the sound of the key in the lock in the evening, that from then forward she would sleep alone and that on going to bed, as she did, later than he, after having finished a chapter or the last version of a story, the bed would not now be warm and welcoming but rather freezing cold and silent just as his study would be frozen, his wardrobe, the armchair in the living room, the car seat.

It had taken her a lot to recover. Bureaucracy helped: she told Leo not to worry about her, she would be fine, as soon as their father was discharged he should return to Brazil and she would take care of everything, and that is what she did. She sat down with Moreno and Dellasiega, Ricardo's partners, to talk about money, given that the building in which the practice operated had been bought by the three and was in the name of all three; she took care of the declaration of presumed death; she filed for the pension.

She wasn't writing. She cried at night. She set *Hidden Variables* aside. She reread what she had and recognized its weaknesses: Seguer maintained, and it was fine that way, that women, his character, women were opaque to him and she knew she understood perfectly a man like Seguer—all of them and therefore he who didn't see through Evelynne? She got tangled up in what she was sure had to be revised and then she did the easiest thing: she forced herself to start a book of short stories which she placed (and often forgot) in a folder in a drawer, unfinished. She came to hate that book still in its infancy, but she went back again and again to the stories, went back to the one that seemed to her the best of all of them; but no, she went back to the weakest trying to find something, a sense, a surface, banal as it might be, that might hide what is not spoken, what boils laboriously as if in the cauldron of those witches who spoke to the one who would be king.

One hot and humid afternoon, trying to recover so as to finish once and for all that book of stories that was still a sterile folder without a title, without signs that might catch the attention of those who would read them, that hot afternoon it occurred to her that what she was doing was an effort that did not lead her to real writing, to that which she had been sharpening by dint of determination and painstaking care and nights in which books, all the books that had been written in the world, spoke to her, only to her.

And then she thought, she knew, that she would have to write a novel that followed the weft of the fabric that spiders weave in shadowy gardens. That, only that, she had no more than that but she sat down to work on what would become *The Ruined Garden*, which had earned her prizes and translations and multiple editions and trips and international colloquia and a lot of money. The other novel, the one about the man who is writing a novel that will remain unfinished, would have to wait and it waited many years. Too many. And now she feels a little sadness, almost remorse, for having left unfinished the novel about the man who can think only of the daughter they took from him, the man who looks for a revolver and a mirror, the man who has been writing a novel he will not finish and about which the one thing he knows is that in the almost round pit, the tomb of the jaguars, his body and hers rot in the darkness, very close to one another.

"I'm leaving, dear, I finished my shift, but don't worry because Blanca is staying in my place. She's going to come clean you up, you know?"

Blanca was like Nelsi, she called her *dear* and sometimes even *treasure* and seemed content with her work. Celina hated to be called *treasure*. The word was too big, it seemed hypocritical, one of those words that hide what they really mean, which is the opposite of what they say. Treasure.

"But, what's the matter?" Emilio had asked her, intrigued. "Why can't I call you my treasure if it's affectionate?"

"I don't like it."

"Bah."

"Yes, bah, but I don't like you to call me that."

It had been one of the first times in the house on the headland that was the safest place to meet without being seen by anyone. The house had been abandoned for years and she found that inexplicable, and so she had asked Emilio why he didn't fix it up since it was a strong, attractive building with a fabulous view of the sea.

"It barely needs anything more than a few superficial repairs and it would be fantastic."

But he said no, he had plenty with taking care of the apartment, the house in the country that had belonged to his parents, and the other one, the one where Ramona lived with the woman who took care of her, because as she was old and deaf and there was no question of taking her to live in the apartment, he had to take care of everything. Another house? Please, no.

It really was too much for him. He was always trying to get anything inessential off his back. Emilio did not come from a family like so many others: people with modest aspirations, immigrant grandparents who had finally bought a house in the neighborhood, cobbled streets, bananas and birds of paradise by the walk, with an outer door and two balconies with iron railings at the front, two patios and kitchen at the back, like her family's or Ricardo's. He came from a family proud of its names, its lands, houses, and travels. Of all that, there remained a good quantity of money and another of pride, but no land anymore. The land had been sold little by little and all that had been retained was the big house. Nothing left, either, of those travels that now seemed the stuff of legend and which he said did not interest him, nor had they ever interested him; the world was the same everywhere and there were opportunities everywhere for those who knew how to take advantage of them and pitfalls for those who did not.

Emilio's father, an imposing man, mustache and belly, who seemed to have nothing for his son other than demands and the corrective of the belt buckle *you have to always be the first arrive early not let them screw you win and win by getting ahead of anyone else* and for his two daughters the indifference owed those who will not perpetuate the family name, had died years ago, when Emilio was almost twenty. His mother, beautiful and neurasthenic, had survived her husband, dressed in pastel-hued chiffon and Japanese silks, useless for anything other than going into debt playing whatever was at hand and crying from time to time over her lost past as a lyric soprano, which Emilio always suspected came bearing exaggerations, and died as soon as he had left home.

He lived alone for a time and three or four years later he married a rich girl and used part of her money and part of his own in ruinous businesses until he found what was best for him. With the restaurant chain it had finally gone as his father had wished, almost incredibly well. It had been a long time since he had heard anything of his sisters. They had fought over jewelry and crystal and paintings as soon as their mother was dead and one of them, he didn't know which one, now lived in Paris and the other who knows where. He had a lot, too much, with the three houses in his charge, and he did not even want to hear about one more house.

The one on the headland was a big stone building, almost at the edge of the cliff, cool in summer and freezing in winter. When it was very cold, Emilio took two or even three blankets and an electric heater and she took a thermos of hot coffee and the tuna sandwiches he liked.

There was no danger. The house was far from the road, separated from any place where people lived, hidden by a tangled fence of trees, vines that climbed up the trunks and wild plants that grew at their feet. It was a naked house, without garden or patio or paths or beds of flowers, surrounded only by uneven gravel planted with pebbles that made the going difficult and held no tracks of those who had walked that way. The glass in the windows had been broken by stones thrown by boys playing on the beach, by people who had lost their way, by the odd vagabond who had tried to get in. Inside there were bird's nests in a few rooms but there were no rats nor any of the disagreeable creatures that slither, nor of the four-footed furry ones with little red eyes.

It had a tower she had never climbed, *it's dangerous*, Emilio said, *the staircase is falling to pieces and it doesn't have a railing*. It had neither galleries nor balconies.

The heart of the house was a room with eight sides, almost round, with four doors, one in every other wall, that led to different parts of the house: one to the bedrooms, one to the dining room and the kitchen, another to something Emilio called the winter garden, and the last to an interior patio that held the staircase leading to the tower. It had no windows, an advantage in the winter months. And in the summer it was the coolest part of the house.

They met there at least once a week and often twice. He was always the first to arrive. They left their cars hidden between the house and the edge of the cliff and entered through the kitchen opening the door with heavy antique keys of storiated iron. They embraced, speaking mouth against mouth, he examined her, eyes closed, hands eager, and they entered the octagonal room in which there was a bed, two chairs, a table, the heater in the winter, and where they spent the rest of the day and, if they could, part of the night.

With the morning, the wall of the building over there across the avenue had gone back to being gray, stained, uninhabited, mute as any wall of any building.

"The doctor on call is coming, dear. I'll change your IV and wash you before he arrives," said Blanca, "it's Doctor Hernández, do you remember him? He hasn't come in two weeks or so, he was at a course at the Central Hospital, you know? Be careful, that's it, slowly, don't make the needle move because then we have a problem afterward, and that's with you having good veins, thank goodness, because sometimes, you can't imagine, there are people where you just don't know how to insert the needle. There he comes, wait while I raise your bed a little, I can't raise the back a lot because Doctor Quirós says no, but a little won't do you any harm, good morning, doctor."

Too bad it was daytime. Too bad because the golden landscape disappeared. Doctor Hernández, a short, skinny, good-looking guy with pretty eyes and ears that were a little big, told her the phlebotomist was going to come because they had to do another blood test. She said fine, thinking about Emilio, who also had beautiful eyes, only his were black. Those of Doctor Hernández were light, she couldn't tell whether green or gray. What would Doctor Hernández think if she asked him *doctor are your eyes green or gray?* He imagined her smile was to show her acceptance of the blood tests.

"That's how I like it," he said and gave her little pats on the hand, the right hand, to keep her from moving the left.

Emilio didn't give her pats on the hand: he dragged her to the bed as soon as they entered the octagonal heart of the house on the headland and there was between them a long, exhausting game of caresses and requests and indecent concessions and perverse kisses and moans until she felt she wouldn't be able to endure one second longer his hands on her belly and then she cried or tried to get out of the embrace and then he laughed.

"Don't laugh," she said.

But he kept laughing, hard, and he told her he loved it when she got mad at him and then, only then, did he throw himself on top of her or mount her on top of himself. He would doze but she got up, she leaned on an elbow and looked at him. For a long time, she thought he was beautiful. For a long time, she thought she was going to be able to keep him, that months and years would pass and they would keep going to the house on the headland, they would enter the octagonal, almost round room and throw themselves onto the bed in a hurry, tearing at each other's clothes, dropping whatever they carried in their hands.

It had been nearly half a year of meetings in the old house cleared of stones almost at the edge of the headland and so much passion, so much adventure, so much amazement caused by the two superimposed lives she had to live because she wanted to, because she needed them, because she felt they were what belonged to her, all gave Celina energy and enthusiasm to write as never before, in a torrent, desperately. Sometimes, when Emilio had one of his fits of rage, not about her but with life, the business, what he called betrayals that came down to disagreements or differences of opinion with the people who surrounded him in his other life, the one Celina didn't share, instead of being frightened, she contemplated him with an almost childish emotion, with a disturbance of spirit similar to the one that flooded her when the idea for another novel was hatching within her. Like someone who is suddenly before an unexpected landscape that doesn't lack for dangers yet which it is necessary to enter so as to feel how life runs in the blood, how the chest expands, how the diaphragm rises during the race, how the eyes fill with a new light and one sees for the first time the world just as the gods created it, out past the garden of Eden.

The phlebotomist was neither skinny nor handsome and who knows about his eyes because he wore the thick glasses of the hopelessly nearsighted. Nor did he give her little pats on the hand, just a good morning and,

"Let's see, hon, straighten your arm, close your hand tight, breathe deeply, all done, you can open your hand," and he left.

Years hadn't passed; months, maybe, four or five, no more. She hadn't fixed on the dates, hadn't made calculations or settled accounts nor had she thought, *It's all over*. And it was, it was all over; what to her had seemed eternal had dissipated in an abyss hung with words that came from the dark corners of the man with whom she had gone to bed in the house on the headland over the course of—how long? What did it matter? Too much time, too little, too much. She was left with a pain like a burn, like a scorched body in which any touch, even that of the air, awakened an unbearable torment. She was left with the certainty that what she had done was the only thing possible. Also another certainty, that no one would ever know who it had been. Sometimes she dreamt, facing the blank page, that someone figured everything out and confronted her with that moment. But it was almost a game: she knew, because she had dealt with that very carefully, she knew it wouldn't happen, that no one would find out.

"Do you remember Lescano?" Ricardo asked.

"Who?"

"Lescano, tall guy, dark, very pleasant. I introduced him to you at Adolfo and Lurecia's."

"You did? I don't remember."

"Yes, Emilio Lescano, I think he's a relative of Lucrecia's, owner of a restaurant chain."

"Oh, right, I think so. Why?"

"They found him dead in an abandoned house close to the beach. They shot him three times."

"Poor man, how awful."

Blanca came in to tell her they were going to give her a very tasty breakfast, that's what she said, very tasty, tea with milk and toast with jam. She said she wanted coffee.

"Oh, no, not coffee. Doctor Quirós said tea with milk. But the nutritionist is going to come later and you ask her if they can let you have coffee. Be a little patient, treasure, here comes the maid."

When everything was over and she was once again alive and attentive to her novels—which one had she been writing at that time, settled at the unpolished wooden table in her workroom? Maybe *The Hostages*, no, no, long before that, *Misunderstandings*, had it been *Misunderstandings*, or *The*

Novaress? It didn't matter, some novel, between *White Sea* and *The Ruined Garden*. When everything was over, while she forced herself to forget, she was sure of one thing and that was that she had never liked the house on the headland and she had liked even less the octagonal room in which she had gone to bed with Emilio once a week and twice when they could. It was sinister, a windowless hole, all of it dark and the shadowy ceiling that seemed to throw itself on top of them, squash them like in that story—who was it by?—in which the character starts to guess they're going to suffocate him between the bed and the ceiling when he sees a picture in which the hat, the wig, the head of the man silk slippers sword at his belt obsequious smile lace gloves are disappearing little by little. The character in the story—the one who was sleeping in that bed that was not his own, not the figure in the painting—escaped in time. She did too. But that dark cavity had lingered, it had remained in her memory with an inexplicable persistence. Inexplicable? She had lived a secret, heart-rending life in the room so octagonal it was almost round, that room that was like a spider with its eight legs, each one on a wall, that room that was like a tomb and had ended up being a tomb. There were no windows, light did not enter, the air was damp and heavy and she imagined that when they left, their smells, their breath, their sweat, all their respiration and the murmur, all the air of all the gestures remained suspended in the frozen space, condensed against the walls, creaking in the wood of the doors. Maybe it was that and not the powerful darkness of every day that turned it into a tomb, but a tomb that would be the final step of a torment impossible to put into words, the torment of a spider bite transformed from a ballerina's shadow into an iron maiden. A tomb, yes, but also a space of past metallic noises that could take one by surprise, just because, because at night, everyone knows, if sleep does not defend a person, if she watches the night awake, then she hears the voices of agony, the bellow of the floods, the rockslide of boulders that tumble off the cliffs, the iron—white, it's so red—that pierces the flesh, the executioner's laugh, the babble of the madman, the prayers of those who die on the rack.

Why not? Why wouldn't places like that one store the world's voices? But not all of them, no, only those that have resonated in the dark, secret, almost subterranean sites scattered over the earth in which neither the sun nor hope can fit, in which one only waits for death.

But she had been happy in that cold, dark room. Had she? She thought so, thought what she had felt for Emilio—and maybe, now and then, what Emilio had felt for her— sketched a different sign on the rough walls, killed the smell of enclosure, washed the horror from that ill-omened ceiling. She no longer even knew; she wanted to go on believing it had been so.

Sad chamber, cursed house, and it wasn't that she was sorry; indeed, she repented of nothing. Maybe he was beautiful but he was contemptible, and she had enjoyed herself immensely in that bed in that room in that stone house, and so what? She had also had a marvelous time with Ricardo in the first years of marriage and with Juan Manuel in the apartment on 2 de Septiembre. And Juan Manuel was also beautiful, although a different type, and he was absurdly young and she knew from the beginning it wasn't going to last and it didn't last but she didn't care. With Emilio, she did care.

"Coffee?" said the nutritionist. "Well, there's no harm as long as it's no more than one cup a day, maybe at the evening coffee hour, does that seem all right to you?"

"Of course," said Celina. "Will you tell the nurse?"

The nutritionist said yes, of course, she would leave the order in the office.

She fooled herself for a time, weeks, almost a month, thinking it was nothing, it did not matter that she now arrived long before he did and would have to wait for him, he was a busy man, loaded with responsibilities and deals and of course he couldn't arrange all his time the way she could. But she knew something was going on and she refused to put a name to that something. There was a void made of time that to her appeared blank, a lack of watchwords, a delay in the arrival of envelopes with the letterhead of societies of arts and letters, but when at last they met again at the house on the headland, everything was as it had always been. *Always* was a word that lacked all meaning. There is no always, there is no then, there is no after. What there was between them was a time, concrete and hanging, suspended and stretched until it almost broke to pieces and in that time, as if on a stage, Emilio sent her messages inside innocent envelopes in plain view of anyone, or she called him in the name of Señorita Yolanda to let him know she had the liquidation lists ready. It was when they met that time assumed its customary dimensions and there was a *then* and there was after and she could calculate, but did not want to, the dimensions of what was happening with Emilio. He was still beautiful, they still hurried, almost running to reach the octagonal room but less every time and every time with fewer words until Celina stopped writing and reading and thinking so as to spend the mornings and the afternoons, arms crossed as if she were cold, walking through the house, going up the stairs, going down, opening doors, closing them, going out to the patio, looking out the windows, turning on the lights, turning them off, leaning against a wall, *my food rots / the chairs spin / the lamps melt / the sheets catch fire / the eggs shatter / the mirrors grow old / the blinds close on me / the walls agonize / and I am alone in the house* trying to fix her gaze on something, a picture frame, a lamp, the latch on the door into the kitchen, so as to study it, describe it, deny everything that did not belong to that metal, that glass, that wood, that thing devoid of anything that was not its very existence clinging to what it could not cease to be.

Nothing mattered too much; she didn't even miss leaning on her elbow, half covered by the blanket, watching him sleep and telling herself he was beautiful. What did matter was that she was no longer writing. She covered up the longing with the excuse, *I want him to be happy.*

She saw, suddenly, when the house (her house, not the one on the headland) was becoming an underground jail it was impossible to get out of and in which she could only contemplate the useless existence of objects, she saw, understood, that Emilio was someone else, distinct from the man she met once or twice a week in the room without windows. He had, she imagined, smooth striped suits hanging in a wardrobe and slippers and handkerchiefs in the drawers, and habits she did not know and refusals that found no place when they were together. She hesitated when she came to think he was a stranger, but she knew that in fact it was so: it wasn't a matter of a character in her novels, he was there and she could not manage him even abiding by everything she had learned, even knowing everything she knew about him, everything that was there inside as if his flesh had been transparent to the light of an internal sun; knew those bursts of lightning she had managed to see when they barely reverberated in a black sky of black eyes and skilled hands were also that man who attacked her, who called her *my treasure* to make her mad, who fled from her even though he remained beside her, who plotted reprisals or had tough answers to questions she had barely asked, if she had even done that much.

"I want him to be happy," she said aloud to the mirror in the living room. "If it's necessary, I'll suggest we separate for a time. Maybe that's what he needs, that we go a while without seeing each other."

"If you need a little time . . ." she said.

"What I need is money," said Emilio.

Surprise left her speechless. Money? what about money? what was up with the money, why? what was this man telling her? And then he proposed something that, maybe because it was what was tormenting him, made him narrow his eyes and grind his teeth as he said it to her and in addition, as a part of something she was not able to understand, he told her it was urgent, he told her that, urgent; and also, moved by something that she, incredibly, did not recognize and of which she had seen only those lightning bursts, he told her he had let an opportunity to resolve it pass only because he knew she was waiting for him in the house on the headland and if she wanted to keep seeing him, she had to get it by next Thursday.

Celina thought of Lot's wife and felt exactly, she knew it was so, that it was exactly what that woman had felt on the road while she was dying, hard and white, crumbled over the bones that until then had held her up.

She, who was not that other one, felt how her toes hardened, the nails fell off, her skin became wrinkled, the pleats of her knees and elbows and ankles were erased, salt flooded her mouth and the crystal grains grew in place of her teeth, a different world, all white, entered her through her eyes, her heart stopped beating, and air no longer reached her lungs but she kept living and hearing, further and further away, the voices of the people who surrounded her and were probably saying something to her that now she did not understand but with the little strength she had left, she agreed and tried to act as if she were the same woman as always, the one of flesh, blood, humors, skin and soul and voice, the one who spoke and breathed and laughed and ate and walked on her feet.

For a moment, while driving home, she thought she was lost, that her life, broken as if it had been made of glass, was falling down around her and she could do nothing to prevent it. But it was only a moment. The cry of triumph of the deity that flew above the unlikely pedestal of Samothrace let her know there was no way out. Or if there was, it was the one and only exit. She shook the salt from her hair and her eyes, moved her hands over the steering wheel to be sure it obeyed her, breathed in all the air in the world, her heart started beating again, and although she remained frozen on the inside, hard and quiet, immobile as if having lost all capacity for movement, she knew she was alive and that she had a week's respite and that in the seven day pause she would set herself to learning how to cultivate a passion born of another, that other one that was the one she had suppressed until she made it the keeper of a nameless happiness that seemed to have had a limit: the impossibility of writing. It only seemed so. That other that was taking shape would be her salvation.

The road was favorable: a gray track, straight, that ran through the middle of a flat landscape in which there were neither houses nor hills; only from time to time a lake or animals grouped around a drinking trough. And if she left things to resolve on their own? If she did nothing, said nothing? Ricardo wouldn't be able to believe it, but if he did believe, ah, then there is a then and there is an after and there is an always in which she wouldn't be able to write either. She needs that tranquility of knowing everything is in its place, people and things and gestures and words. Illusory calm: everything is so precarious, so much so that one day it will be undone by cold and nothing will remain, not even the memory of the words spoken; but yes, something will remain, yes, something, the words written, because although there may be no one to read them, they will be there and they will continue to mean something. And if someone reads them who doesn't know the language she writes in, well then they'll have a different meaning, the way the ideogram of the horse had for the old poet.

Everything she imagines, the solitude, the drama, the abandonment, the inability to write, none of it happens that way in her life. It only happens in fantasy and in desire. And she, settled there, can—should—make a decision that will not be, certainly, to let the difficult period, the crisis and the choice flow out into an arid land that will never nourish her and in which she will die helplessly of hunger and thirst.

She will not allow it. The woman of salt, standing up in the middle of the gray road, knows and she knows it as well, the two of them elbow to elbow, survivors of verdicts and bribes, knows they will not allow it. Nor will there be goodbyes or demands, let alone complaints or reproaches.

The air becomes heavier as she reaches the city. There's wind: it won't rain tonight. But she has already been able to assure herself that for so much disruption, so many open roads that lead nowhere, there is only one solution; she knows the order of the world is there, within reach of her hand.

At midday, the wind shook the crowns of the trees and after having lunch—if you could call what the nutritionist instructed them to give her lunch—she slept half an hour because she couldn't get rid of *the doctor's little pill, treasure.* She had visitors: smiling friends, Robi who told her clumsily that Leo was going to come see her, well, he wasn't coming because of her, he said, but because he had to come and would stop to see her on the way, Pepe Maderna and his wife and Enriqueta Méndez who was writing a thesis on *The Hostages.* Quirós came in with two other doctors she had not seen before and they asked questions and looked at the chart that hung at the end of the bed and went away full of smiles. The afternoon stretched out more than it should. She drank broth and water and another little pill that she spat out in time and night fell and the golden landscape appeared on the smooth, stained, hard wall of the building beyond the avenue.

She looked for the little gray spider but it had disappeared. *It can't be,* she almost said aloud, *it has to be somewhere.* But the shadow of the little spider wasn't so important, not enough to make her look in other corners: what she wanted was to go back to seeing the gold on the wall beyond the avenue, the gold, the honey, the wheat, the amber and tortoiseshell light; to lay her eyes on the landscape now without thinking how she could write that, only looking, question and pleasure, that which made her live again, made her deny death, to know that a second is as long as the long history of the world, that she had before her all the time there was, time meager yet heavy with meaning, with voices, with iron or foam under the fingers, with the beneficent light.

She would not think again about what she had lost, Ricardo's body sinking in the shadowy sea, the novels she would not write, the soft, almost feminine, clumsy hands of

Juan Manuel, Emilio's smile when he told her he needed that sum, that what Ricardo had earned with the Donatti inheritance was double what he wanted and either she got it or Ricardo found out everything, Juan Manuel included, positions, whims, small perversions—small like the little gray spider, strong like the silvered thread hung in the sun, sticky and invincible—details and words of the charged air in the room without windows.

It didn't matter anymore. If the memory of sorrow is the sorrow, then she had no memories and what was coming back was only a scene that did not belong to her and perhaps had never belonged to her, foreign and played by others, never, not entirely, by her; she had freed herself from everything and the only thing she wanted was to drink coffee at the evening coffee hour and at night look at the past gold, undecipherable, ripe as the fruits of summer trees that shone beyond the avenue, for her, only for her.

Somewhere in this world that beats like a cruel and magnificent heart, Johnny Keats had a cold drink and ate avocado with pepper and lemon. From Saverio, he never heard anything ever again. Maurois sat with him in the afternoons in the Café de la Piragua and they talked while watching, smelling the sea. With the cargo arrived books that he or the doctor had ordered and which they gave to each other afterward although they weren't entirely interested in the same things. For Maurois, history; for Johnny, discoverers of whatever it might be but above all anthropology and physics. And for both of them, the recounting of the two world wars. Maurois from time to time ordered some book about art because he had discovered Gheeraerts reading the lives of Anne Boleyn and her daughter, or Berruguete when he learned about the works and days of the dukes of Urbino.

They didn't talk about women. Each had their secrets that each knew were not really secret. Johnny knew something of Maurois' past history because Maurois himself had told him, and he knew, as the whole island knew, that Ruth Humao went to the house every Friday without fail and they shut themselves in until Sunday night; but the doctor was still unaware, or pretended to be unaware that Johnny had overcome amnesia and remembered his other life. Why talk about that, if life was the one he was living now, a life that belonged entirely to him, in which he could condense, possess, keep to himself everything that assailed him, from the desires to the nightmares, without regrets, with no need to justify himself to anyone or offer himself explanations.

Under Maurois' tolerant smile, back in the first days of the first shadows of the first near memories, he had decreed that no, it would not be possible for him, oh no, never would he go to bed with a native woman. For that reason, he had been hanging around Inez Romero, a haughty girl with a narrow waist, dressed almost always in white, fan and sunglasses in her hand. He invited her for a drink or an outing to the mountains and she sometimes accepted and sometimes no, and sometimes neither yes nor no, saying her mother needed her at home. Maurois asked him one night how the romance was going and Johnny protested, what romance was he talking about, progress was very slow, there was no romance yet. Maurois told him there would be none. And there was not.

When Náyade Saluga crossed his path, the first thing he did was ask himself how it was that he had not seen her before. And the second was to go to bed with her.

From then on life was much, much easier. Náyade was a queen. She did not know how to read or write but she carried her chin high, she didn't move her arms when she walked, she dressed however she pleased, in colored tunics or European-style or in twill trousers and a linen shirt, she painted only her eyelids, in purple, and sometimes a beauty-mark on her right cheek, in black. She didn't know how to cook or sew or iron or clean or make the bed, but she found from the other side of the mountains a woman who would cook and on this side a girl for the other chores. She never raised her voice to them: she taught them to gather their hair under a scarf, to say yes ma'am and yes sir and thank you and please, to use an apron and to wash their hands when they touched something in the kitchen or in the bathroom.

She never wanted to live in the house that had belonged to Saverio. She stayed in the house on Ferrán Street where she had lived, she said, with her husband. It was rumored on the island that the man who had arrived with her was not legally her husband, but that didn't matter much to anyone. He was ill; Náyade took care of him, she helped him to walk as far as the gallery and sit in the afternoon sun, she gave him his medicines, called the doctor when necessary. More necessary every time, and more and more frequently, until the man died, silently, with a certain effort, just as he had lived.

She buried him and the next day, carrying a wooden box with a bronze latch, she went to the bank and opened an account in her own name. Some six months later she went to bed with Johnny as has been noted and a year or more after that, he rented a decent house for her facing the plaza. She bought a new bed and armchairs for the living room and lamps and rush mats; he gave her a hammock. She accepted gifts but never wanted him to pay her bills.

When she went home in the morning or arrived in the evening, Johnny looked at the coppery skin of her arms or her not-so-narrow waist or the throat rising proudly from the neckline of her tunic or the lace of her blouse, and understood that smile of Maurois'. And that even though, he was sure, Ruth Humao was not as beautiful as Náyade.

One-eyed Miguel no longer fished. Overcome by rheumatism, he sat at another table of the Café de la Piragua and wrapped his misshapen hands around the glass of gin the Portuguese Basilio passed him. He spoke to them from time to time and complained of pains in his knees and his wrists.

"Come to the hospital and I'll give you a painkiller," Maurois said.

And Johnny, "Relax, don Miguel. You have children and grandchildren who now go out to fish and let you want for nothing."

"It was the sea," said Miguel Toro, "that fog that rises and grabs you, wrings all the blood out of you, that was it, the sea."

Maurios and Johnny stopped paying attention to him and ended the day eating in Mimosa's bar out past the lighthouse, or at Johnny's house where Náyade would preside over the table and keep an eye on the servants.

"I'm leaving," Maurois said before midnight. "I have to be at the hospital early."

They said goodbye. Johnny closed the door, turned off the lights, drank a glass of warm milk and lay down to sleep alone or with his arms around the robust copper woman. He didn't dream, or at least he didn't remember, if he had dreams, what faces, what winds, what tricks and intrigues he had seen in them.

She saw him again in the middle of the week:

"Señorita Yolanda speaking," she said.

She felt so calm, almost happy, certain that in the future she would be able to write as much as she wanted, that the longing would return, the objects in her house would once again have the appropriate and perfect consistency given them by the slow time of the clocks and the frugal scratching of the pen over the paper. What she did not feel was fear. Not of the dark things that emerge from the pits of memory, nor of losing the forest of words in which she felt she had been born, nor that something or someone might separate her from the life she wants, that she always wanted.

"What did you get?"

"Nothing, nothing yet, but I wanted to know if it couldn't wait one more week."

"You made me come out here for that? I already told you no. Thursday, Thursday, understood?"

"Very well."

He pushed her and made her fall down on the bed. Afterward he did not doze off. He dressed hurriedly, went to the door, the one that led to the kitchen through which they always entered, he went through it and closed it behind him. With the lock.

"What's going on?" she yelled. "What's happening? Why did you lock me in?"

He didn't answer. There was silence on the other side of the door and the silence lasted—how long? She didn't know, she didn't have a watch, she wasn't able to calculate if it was hours or minutes, not even counting her own pulse, but she knew she had been mistaken: there was not one and only one way out but rather at least one more, this one, unexpected.

But the thing is, she didn't want to; she didn't want to die for lack of air closed up in that tomb so octagonal, it was almost round. And since she didn't want to, for a moment she was at the brink of something close to panic. Her legs wobbled and she wanted to go to the bed to sit down but she couldn't. It wasn't fear, no, not that fear of finding behind the wardrobe door something black with eyes and a smell of damp. Cold sweat spilled down her forehead and over her face. She ran her tongue over parched lips; her teeth were clenched together top and bottom and on the back of her neck a tickle, but not from spiders, not from spiders. That was not, it could not be fear. *Enough*, she said in a very low voice in case Emilio was on the other side of the closed, locked door trying to hear something, *enough*. Enough, and that was sufficient. She could walk, breathe deeply, very deeply. She sat on the bed and waited because she knew, she thought she knew, that there could be another way out. She didn't think about light or about air, nor about Ricardo nor about sitting down again to write at the unpolished wooden table in her armchair upholstered in crimson.

She thought instead about how the velvet was a little worn, true, but she would take it to be reupholstered. Of course, she wouldn't like sitting in a regular chair or in another armchair while the upholsterer fixed it up. She liked her own chair, which had been hers for so long. She thought for a long moment about the crimson velvet, a little worn.

She was thinking about that and deciding it would be dark green if the same shade of crimson could not be found when Emilio opened the door, smiling.

"Were you scared?"

"Of course not," she said.

"It was a joke, my treasure."

"I know."

"And by the way we know how things stand between the two of us, right? We know."

"Of course we know," she smiled as well.

Might the golden landscape be a vision of paradise? Elvira dressed in white, Elvira whom she had never met, passed in front of her eyes just as if she had been present, young, happy as Ricardo had told her she looked. When she learned of Ricardo's death, Celina tried to locate her so as to let her know. But at the convent they told her she was no longer there, they had transferred her. She asked where to and they said they were unable to tell her.

"But it's important. I want to tell her that her brother has died."

"Sister Constancia does not have a brother. She long ago renounced all worldly things," they told her and that was all.

At least she had found out what Elvira's name was behind the convent walls. Constancia, Sister Constancia, what would Ricardo have said about that?

Señorita Yolanda called to inform that the liquidation lists were ready. The secretary told her she would inform Señor Lescano immediately.

Now that she had something to compare it to, she understood that it had been easier than swallowing the little pill from Doctor Quirós, treasure. And she remembered, that night she had slept peacefully, without dreaming. Ricardo had arrived late and they had eaten she didn't remember what, and she had washed the dishes in the kitchen and had left them in the sink because the next day Marta would come to clean; meaning that since Marta came Monday, Wednesday, and Friday, that would have been a Tuesday or a Thursday, yes, possibly a Thursday.

The revolver was a short .38 with mother-of-pearl grips that had belonged to her father and that neither Leo nor Robi had wanted. They advised her to throw it in the river. A weapon in the house is dangerous, they told her, and she agreed. She took the box of bullets too, not because she thought someday she was going to shoot bullets with that revolver but because she thought it was the two things together, complete, that she had to be rid of.

Two days later she said she had thrown it away but it wasn't true: she had kept it, she wasn't very sure why, always thinking that yes, of course she was going to throw it in the river but not today, maybe tomorrow, or Saturday; she kept it and saved it wrapped in a chamois cloth along with the round tin box. It was put away back where the mementos of first loves are stored or identity documents no longer in use or some old piece of jewelry that isn't very valuable and even a sepia photograph of who knows who anymore, maybe a grandmother or somebody's mother or maybe the second wife of someone else: in the third drawer of the closet beneath the lingerie. There was no longer any danger that the twins would rummage through her wardrobe and it wouldn't even occur to Ricardo to open her drawers and look inside.

Emilio was smiling and friendly, even affectionate. Not passionate like other times, affectionate. So much that she thought it was a shame. He asked if she had gotten it. She looked at him as if in that first dreaminess, when one doesn't know yet but feels there is something stretching from one to the other and that something is solid and is going to resist the storms.

"Get what?" she said.

"Come on! We both know what."

He said it with some impatience but also, she thought, with a trace of fear.

She laughed, no dreaminess, "Yes, of course. I was thinking," she said while she searched through her purse, "that we could go away somewhere for a weekend. Yes, I already know what you're going to say, but who knows? Neither Ricardo nor your wife would suspect and, oh, let's see, it's a long time now that I've wanted to go to the beach with you for ten days, a week, three days, I don't know, the little time we have, yes, here it is."

Emilio suppressed his smile—he didn't need it now, anyhow —and waited. Celina took the revolver out of her black purse, aimed, and shot.

"Three shots? But that's horrible," she said. "Did they catch the killer?"

"Seems not," Ricardo said, looking over the paper, "let's see, continued on page seventeen third column, no, they found the body because they saw the car abandoned on the side of the road, if it hadn't been for that, years could have gone by without anyone realizing something had happened there. They searched the grounds some, there's a high fence. Behind it there's a house, an old stone house, that had the door standing open; they went in and they found him. There are no clues. They'll never catch them, they must have gone to rob him and the car wouldn't start so they left on foot or who knows, maybe a motorcycle. There are no footprints because apparently the house is in the middle of rocky ground. What did he go out there for, I wonder?"

"Who knows?" Celina said. "Shall I pour you more coffee?"

"No, that's fine, I'm leaving now, I'm running late. What are you going to do today?"

"Those people from the cultural supplement, from the newspaper, are coming to interview me, and then I'll stay in and work."

"I won't be home for lunch, okay?"

"Fine."

Then she had written *The Novaress*. Yes, she thought so, almost certainly *The Novaress*. She was pleased with that novel. She hadn't read it again because, once it was published, she never reread what she had written. But it was a good novel: she had achieved a certain oppressive atmosphere, almost sinister, and the characters had a sufficient dose of mystery to allow the readers to imagine that what was suspected but wasn't said, was true. It had been well received by the critics and had sold quite well, enough to let them remodel the house and buy her a new car, without having to use up all the money on those two things.

Somewhere, someone was playing a piano: one, two, three almost hesitant notes, as if stammering; on further thought, maybe it was a children's song, a round; how strange, she had never heard a piano there. The sound had, she was sure of it, some relation to the golden landscape. It could be, who knows, the murmur that was missing, a murmur that would not come from fountains but from the uncertain scales of a piano. She let herself go—eyes closed—in the music and the nurse, Nelsi again, looked in and thought *she's asleep, poor thing, better not bother her, I'll come back in a while.*

She wasn't sleeping. She knew she wasn't sleeping, she knew she was not falling asleep, because whether or not she had taken the little pill—so tiny dear with a little swallow of water—sleep was something else: sleep was that second, less than a second in which the body becomes heavier and seeks in the sheet the mattress the bed the room the house the entire universe, heavens included, a slice of world in which to fit without effort. Those who sleep, those who are falling asleep, hardly know it is the body that becomes wise and allows them to sleep. They barely perceive that passage from wakefulness into shadow because it is the body that lowers their eyelids and measures their breathing.

Celina wasn't sleeping. Her arms and her waist and her knees were still busy forgetting the place they had filled when awake. And she who wasn't sleeping was occupied not with places nor with the bulge of her belly or the hollow below her throat but with her life.

Slowly, as if unintentionally, life claimed her now that death was closer than she believed. She could not know—because no one gets to know that and news of death comes swelling through the air from the cities in the heavens—that she had to hurry, that life held her but the golden light was blinding her and would make her, at last, close her eyes.

Meanwhile, she bit into the apple of childhood. Her sharp, white, sweet teeth entered the flesh—white and sweet and round—and a few drops of juice rolled down her gums. Her tongue passed over her lips, yes, all the way around, like the oooh of a girl's mouth. Her fingers trapped it, soft and curved like the dreams she had dreamed and she bit and bit again, she bit the rage, the hard rock that had settled in her chest forever after having fired three times in the jaguars' tomb, until the little pips got between the biting and the tasting and she had to pull her tongue back toward her palate, find the small roughness that was the word against which she was struggling and which she sometimes overcame and sometimes not and that she could finally expel from her mouth and her fingers and from the disturbance of spirit with a *pfff* and her tongue that went over her mouth and the mouths, one by one, of the men that she had loved and that waited for her when it coiled around her upper lip, her tongue, like another being, faintly pink and alive, demanding she bring it the taste of everything that surrounded her, whatever it might be, happiness or a wandering lie or crossroads or misfortune.

She threw the bitten, worthless core of the apple into the garbage and from there below the rancid smell of the kitchen scraps assailed her and her nose filled with a breath of something dead like the breathing, murmurs, sweat that were left in the eight-sided room or in the always disordered apartment or beside the unpolished wooden table from which had been born the useless dead, her own or someone else's, that asked what use was death if not to write it and add a definite knowledge to what cannot be lived. A knowledge that suffocated her just as if air had turned to slow, cushioned footsteps, dense and yellow, unbreathable, impossible to accept. Quickly quickly, before it took over her mouth and her breathing, she closed the almost full container that she or her mother would take out to the sidewalk that night, and breathed the white hopeful scent of clean in the cupboard with the soaps and the floor mops and brushes and sponges while her father opened the newspaper and the black ink from its fragile pages took the lead over all there is to smell in a house where people live eat read sleep go out come in, a tiny wind that filters through the moving doors and brings the laziness of summer, the sadness of winter, the nights when a storm threatens and one bundles up and feels every little piece, every inch of one's skin and of one's tempted body, announcing that it is there, against all that warms and protects.

The black ink of the newspaper smells like the classroom to which one carries the untippable Bakelite inkwell, only there it was with a heavy smell of pencil, of princesses who live in castles in the clouds, of the wood pencil shavings that fall through one's hands when they're sharpened, of the pass of the water truck, of the white smocks, of the clothes stored in wardrobes until the cold comes back again. Do books smell like the doors of paradise? Yes. Do the wood floors creak like the cicadas in the trees during January siestas? Yes, of course they do with the *rr* of iridescent elytrrrrons that are part of the heavens that cover us. Does the wood of the Faber number 2 pencil smell the same as the wood in colored pencils? Yes. No. The wood in colored pencils smells of orange more than wood and she knew, she knew that what entered through her nose and sank down to her palate when she went to school was different from what entered through her nose and changed in a sweet mouth when she walked down the cobbled street surrounded, lined by tall gray and always silent houses, or when she was in the house where she did that very thing, that, the biting or crying or wetting her hair in the shower or sitting on the rug or reading or collecting silk flowers, or in the amusement park where no matter where you are, you go around and around again and again always at the point of falling into the black void in which Satan opens his hand and the five points of the star become the eight feet of the spider that dances in the garden in the half-light.

She would have been able to close her eyes the way she closes them now, even though the gold landscape disappears when she closes her eyes, and let them take her to school or to the house and say I am at home or I am at school. Then she would open her eyes, she would open them, she opens them now and feels more than she sees the golden light that comes from over there beyond the avenue, and she would see that she had been right, she had always been right in everything she had done and written and felt because through her eyes and her nose, and her mouth and the skin on the tips of her fingers, all the colors come in, and of course the distance but above all the letters that are also of gold although everyone might tell her they are black, which is impossible. If they were black they would not be able to form words and the words do come in through her eyes and her ears and her fingers and her teeth. She eats them at two in the morning when everyone has found their space in the world and sleeps there not wanting to know what calls them from the other side of sleep, not wanting to wake up to reply, because it is not easy to reply when the question has been rolling forward since the first morning of the world, and one life is not enough—only one which is nothing and passes by and is gone—to see it be born. She passes all the words through her mouth, the ones she knows and the ones she doesn't know, the ones that float in the air of the day and of the night, the ones that are used to talk to slaves and to God, all of her mouth like a hole window lake in which to rock them in silence without anyone waking. The guitar of her chest can respond because all that has ever been said or sung resonates there: nothing can be done with the words if they aren't first made to pass through the waist of the guitar, tighten the strings, hear the syllables, support the sonorous body. And afterward, yes, they can be bitten as one bites an apple, they can be touched the way one touches very carefully a warm little animal that gets frightened and runs away if not spoken to softly. One can smell them because the smell comes already placed at the back pole of the mouth when one bites and kisses and talks and cries. The mouth. The heart can rise into the mouth, and it does, oh, how it does when the eyes obey and discover the dot of gold between the faces of two women who try not to look at themselves over the bridge of Saint Bénezet. The mouth. The fingers. Everything that comes in through the arabesques of the tree without end seeking the answers that come in words from the depths of the soul in the form of a bird, rising through the chest, spilling out of the arms, the neck, the fingernails, the flower of the blood. All that is life is going away from her, moving toward the garden of gold that shines only during the nights. The whole palm of the hand, not just the fingers, on the mother-of-pearl grips that aren't cold like metal but warm like that which lives or was once alive, mother-of-pearl, coral, amber, ivory. Like her character, the cold of the metal against the palate, like her at night, knowing both that the act is inevitable and that it comes from an impossible horizon, like the roll of the eyes, the music of a piano, the shadow of the little gray spider that is no longer there, the white that comes to settle on the tunic worn by Elvira, a woman who is only a name, a woman she never saw but who must have smelled of summer, of happiness arduously won.

What is there beyond memory? The globe of the world floating above the shell of a tortoise held up by four eternal elephants? The fruit of knowledge? The hero who descends to the underworld? What was not said because it could not be said? The words that were words before words?

There is only a taste of mint on her lips, chewy candies on the sly, a black cat that meows in the shadows, another tongue against hers in her mouth, skin almost vibrating, the entrance to the forest of what is to be said, the song of what is written. All of her in a whirlwind, attended by the scent, the taste, the touch, the sound of the days and of insomnia. She hands over all of that, hands it over almost happily, knowing it does not belong to her, knowing that everything she has is over there, far away, on the other side of the avenue.

A single desire, to enter the golden landscape, something that would certainly be forbidden but that nonetheless consoles her: to know she can still desire something that she is never going to reach. And in that, flooded with light, the disproportionate minutes slip away, and the hours made of iron like old keys, and the graceful, plotting years of adolescence with the scent of rain when the wind turns and the throat echoes cut grass, dirt streets sprinkled in the evenings, creak of the blinds being closed, voices, the seamless song of the drops on the paving stones, water, always water, the greenish and leafy water of the seas of the beginning of all life that ends in light and explodes in bursts of lightning in the golden garden and leaps like artificial fireworks over everything that ever surrounded her and accompanied her, to leave her only in the moment of taking the step, the wall of an apartment building, smooth and mute beyond the avenue toward which she goes, goes, no longer sleeping—on the contrary, more awake than ever—offered everything she had, what was denied her regained, wrapped in gold, wheat, tortoiseshell, light, the landscape that is surrounding her, bending around her until it forms a crenellation almost round, it's so octagonal, pure brilliance, only walls, eight, luxurious, mild, fragrant with resin, no roof up there above, only a circle that is expanding more and more until it embraces the order of the universe furrowed with threads of silver that sparkle in the sun of the childhood of the world, letting her know, she knows it now, that the eight feet of the spider, the divining points of the star, the exits from the round almost octagonal tomb, are the waves, eight and innumerable, springing from the garden of gold and they envelop her because she no longer has weight or density until her eyes truly close and she sees, now she can see night after night, day after day what returns like perfume, like the maternal waters, like the lucky tears—bluish, taut— of the sea in which perhaps she would have wanted to die, of that sea that once boiled and in which everything, but everything, even gold had begun before time, before the beginning, before fear, before memory, before words.

THE END

AUTHOR'S NOTE

I thank Florencia Balestra for the gracious gift of her text "Esto
no es obra del Señor," 1991, which I have reproduced only in part.

ROSARIO, JANUARY 2003–MAY 2004.

ABOUT THE AUTHOR

Born in Buenos Aires in 1928, Angélica Gorodischer has lived in Rosario since childhood. She is the author of some thirty books, including novels, short story collections, and essays, among them *Bajo las jubeas en flor* (1974), *Trafalgar* (1979), *Mala noche y parir hembra* (1983), *Doquier* (2002), *Tres colores* (2008), *Tirabuzón* (2011), *Palito de naranjo* (2014), *Las nenas* (2016), and *Coro* (2017). Best known outside of Argentina for her works of science fiction and fantasy (*Bajo las jubeas en flor* [1974], *Kalpa Imperial* [1983], and *Trafalgar* [1979]), she has also experimented with crime fiction and memoir, always pushing the boundaries of readers' generic expectations. She studied at the Escuela Normal de Profesoras n° 2 in Rosario and at the then Universidad Nacional del Litoral (now Universidad Nacional de Rosario), but did not complete a degree. She is the recipient of numerous awards, nationally and internationally; she received a Fulbright Fellowship for the International Writing Program of the University of Iowa (1988) and has been a Fulbright Scholar at the University of Northern Colorado (1991); she organized three international meetings of women writers, the Encuentros Internacionales de Escritoras, held in Rosario in 1998, 2000, and 2002. Three of Gorodischer's books have appeared in English translation: *Kalpa Imperial*, translated by Ursula K. Le Guin (2003); *Trafalgar*, translated by Amalia Gladhart (2013); and *Prodigies*, translated by Sue Burke (2015). Gorodischer's short stories have been translated into English, German, French, Italian, Russian, and Czech; *Tumba de jaguares* has been published in German under the title *Im Schatten des Jaguars* (2010).

CPSIA information can be obtained
at www.ICGtesting.com
Printed in the USA
LVHW011940181220
674544LV00004B/223